She Loves Monsters

This special edition of
She Loves Monsters
is limited to 450 numbered copies.

This is number: 394

Simon Clark

SHE LOVES MONSTERS

SIMON CLARK

NECESSARY EVIL PRESS
2006

She Loves Monsters
©2006 by Simon Clark

Artwork ©2006 by Caniglia

Introduction ©2006 by Paul Finch

Design and Layout by David G. Barnett/Fat Cat Design

FIRST EDITION

Published by
Necessary Evil Press
P.O. Box 178
Escanaba, MI 49829
www.necessaryevilpress.com

450 Signed and Numbered Hardcovers
ISBN 0-9753635-4-9
26 Signed and Lettered Deluxe Hardcovers

All rights reserved. No part of this book may be used or reproduced in any manner whatsoever without the written permission of the author.

INTRODUCTION
PAUL FINCH

For anyone who doesn't know Simon Clark, to meet him on a darkened street or in some rowdy, beer-soaked bar can be real a test of nerve. The first impression you get is that you've somehow run into the psycho-killer, Dolarhyde, so spookily portrayed by Tom Noonan in the 1986 horror movie, *Manhunter*. This primarily stems from Simon's height (6'8", at a guess), his lean but strong build, and his penchant for shockingly loud Hawaiian shirts. The second impression you get, however, once you've noted his warm smile and heard his softly-spoken Yorkshire accent, is that he's an all-round good guy who couldn't possibly have an evil bone in his body.

And you'd be wrong on both counts.

Simon Clark certainly isn't a killer, himself. But he has a diabolically devious mind. Over the last 12 years, he's produced some of the scariest, most gruesomely compelling horror fiction of the modern age, his highly original subject-matter always benefiting from well-drawn characters, believable "real world" settings (Simon is usually accurate down to the street names and door numbers of the buildings in which his ghastly events occur), and deeply disturbing subtexts, the memory of which will often linger long after the initial reading experience is over. (And subtext in this instance is what it's all about; believe me, you won't put *She Loves Monsters* down and rest easily afterwards).

I first met Simon in the mid-1990s, at what was loosely termed a "terror scribes do." I was relatively new to the horror-writing game myself, having only had a few short stories published at the time. But I eagerly accepted an invitation to meet a bunch of other northern

SHE LOVES MONSTERS

England-based dark-fantasy authors who were gathering with Simon in a hard-drinking pub somewhere in Sheffield. I went there in a profound state of nervousness, not just because I wouldn't know anyone and would almost certainly feel inferior, but because I wasn't sure how I was going to react to Simon Clark—an idol of mine at the time, and a guy who'd been setting new standards in British horror fiction.

As it turned out, I was made far more welcome than I had any right to expect, particularly by Simon, who was without doubt the star of the show, but to whom the term "airs and graces" would be utterly meaningless. As I recall, we drank together, smoked stacks of cigars, and found that we had enormous tracts of common ground. Both of us were northerners born and bred (and proud of it, in that bolshy, blue-collar way that northerners have), both of us liked our horror earthy and in-yer-face, both of us had deep interests in the mythological undertones of everyday British life, and both of us had an abiding fascination for cinema as a medium, particularly when it came to exploring the darker side of human existence. I remember we spoke at length about plans I had for a horror movie based on my experiences as a copper in Manchester, while Simon also had a number of ideas he one day hoped to put forward for possible film development. We were both firmly of the opinion that, while classic horror literature had originally set us on our chosen paths, the influence of cinema in our lives—not just horror cinema, but any kind of cinema so long as it was dark and subversive—could not be denied, and on the subject of which Simon then asked me a question which kept us busy for much of the rest of the day: did a wannabe film-writer like me believe that the artistically powerful, but at the same time visceral and sordidly violent movies of the late-60s / early-70s have an active role in the development of western society, or were they simply reflecting something that was already happening?

I remember being taken aback by the depth of the enquiry (especially as, between us, we'd by then killed about 26 pints of Yorkshire Best). In some ways, looking back on it, it's almost funny; it seems typical of the sort of pseudo-intellectual subject two well-oiled boozers with artistic pretensions would move onto. But it was a fascinating question all the same, and one that you readers will now need to consider for yourselves, even though at this moment it may seem completely irrelevant to you.

SIMON CLARK

The obvious answer was that I didn't know. How could I know? To this day I don't know. I understood which films Simon was talking about: the likes of *Midnight Cowboy*, *The Devils*, *Straw Dogs*, *A Clockwork Orange*, *The Exorcist* and *Soldier Blue* all exploded from our cinemas at roughly the same time, amid storms of controversy, and when I considered them in a historical context, yes, they were a sort of cultural watershed, a dividing line between the peace-loving but still relatively innocent age of hippy-dom and the aggressive, angst-ridden wasteland that was shortly to follow. Other factors were obviously involved in this apparently abrupt change of social attitudes—political, sociological, psychological, even biological—but the question gnawed at me: did cinema have some responsibility as well, or were the films I've mentioned merely acknowledging (and exploiting!) something that was going on anyway?

For fear of spoiling the grim delights ahead of you in *She Loves Monsters*, I'm not going to elaborate on why I choose to revive this question now. But suffice to say this: of all the art forms on Earth, the movies (often television too, but mainly it's the movies, probably because of their mega-sized impact from the big-screen) stand most accused of exerting unhealthy influences. And it's not just a recent thing. Many undoubted classics from Hollywood's golden age caused a genuine stir on first release: *Citizen Kane* ('41) for its political satire, *White Heat* ('49) for its violence, *From Here To Eternity* ('53) for its steamy love scenes. From the dawn of cinema history, it seems, critics ranging right across the board—from the moral hard-right, to the politically-correct centre, to the censorious hard-left—have been angered by cinema's apparent determination to always challenge convention, to always question the status quo, to always push the envelope of acceptability. But still Simon's question remains: have any of these movies, from past or present, seriously and genuinely altered society on their own? In my opinion, there have been mild examples of cases where they have. *On The Waterfront* ('54) turned America against the mob; *The Searchers* ('56) exploded the myth of the glamorous Old West; *Taxi Driver* ('76) exposed the realities of life in society's urban underbelly. But did they actually change anything? Did they make us go out and do things that previously would have been anathema to us?

Maybe they did and we don't realize it.

SHE LOVES MONSTERS

From the mid-20th century onwards, conspiracy theorists maintained that subliminal advertising was being employed by certain filmmakers, who were being paid by manufacturers to craftily insert single-frame shots of products into their movies, or to decorate their sets with surreptitious brand-naming. Of course, there's no major crime here even if it's true. It's not the end of the world if all we're being manipulated to do is buy a different kind of snack or soda-drink at the intermission.

But just suppose we're being manipulated to do something else?

Suppose the movie in question has been so well made that—either by subconscious promotion, or erudite argument, or maybe a combination of both—it drives home a command of far greater seriousness. We're not zombies, of course, and even under the deepest hypnosis, the average human being can supposedly resist orders to perform acts that he or she would normally find repulsive. But suppose someone some day manages to find a way around even this failsafe system.

You can't deny it. It's a very scary thought.

Now read *She Love Monsters*, and prepare to be chilled in a totally new kind of way.

Paul Finch
June 2005

SHE LOVES MONSTERS
Or The Quest For Lost Vorada

1. EXT. FOREST - DAY
LONG SHOT. A silver BMW speeds along a deserted forest road. The prestige car and the confident driving is the consummate expression of its owner's personality: **I come. I see. I conquer.**

CUT TO:

2. INT. MONTAGE - DAY
UNASSIGNED CAMERA. Camera drifts fluidly through rooms and along corridors decorated with marble statues to find CHRISTOPHER LAKE lying on his bed. Silence—as in a tomb. He stares at the ceiling. It appears we find him moments after his death. An audience APPLAUDS and CALLS out. The EERIE NOTES of an ACCORDION introduce the song AMSTERDAM by Jacques Brel. The MUSIC comes from a laptop computer; on its screen colors oscillate to provide a visual response to VOICE and MUSIC. CHRISTOPHER LAKE slowly blinks to break the appearance of death. He doesn't move, but continues to lie there staring at the ceiling. Camera glides away to exit the room, enter the corridor then drift along, as if this is POV of a spirit visitor. It approaches a window that has views of trees and evening sky. There it stops as the music swells.

CUT TO:

3. INT/EXT. CAR/FOREST - DAY

SHE LOVES MONSTERS

During following CUT between exterior and interior of JACK CALNER'S BMW. MUSIC OVER, continuing seamlessly from scene number 2. AMSTERDAM grows in VOLUME and quickens in pace as JACK CALNER pilots the car along the road as if it's a missile. The epitome of self assurance—this is a man on a quest. Ahead, a sign for a cattle grid. He brakes, not violently, but enough to allow the car to cross the grid in safety…

One

This is the first time I've hit a woman.

She asks for it. I mean, she REALLY does ask for it. In fact, I can't even stop myself. POW! She's sprawling in the dirt. She's rolling over, her arms flung out, hair spilling wildly. And did I tell you she's naked? Not a stitch. Not a thread. Nothing on her bare body but scratches and a bruise the size of an open hand on her gleamingly nude hip.

That's the first time I hit a woman. It happens as I'm driving to a house that's been mine for ten months, but I've never clapped eyes on it, never mind set one foot across its expensive threshold. It's the biggest asset I own. Thank you, Dad, for putting it just beyond reach. Look up the definition of "tantalize" in the dictionary and you'll know the mood I'm in when I strike her down.

I'd been driving for six hours. After passing through the mountains and forests of Cumbria, one of the rare wilderness tracts of England, I'd just had my first teasing glimpse of Montage with its spires, a green dome and red chimneys—my Montage, bequeathed to me in my father's last will and testament. The sun was setting. I could see the red light reflected in the windows like the house—*my house*—was filled with fire.

A sign told me a cattle grid lay ahead, so I braked. A second later the woman ran from the trees onto the road and—**BANG**! I saw her naked body roll up over the hood of the car. Her bare hip struck the windshield, turning it into a spider's web of radiating lines.

SO THIS IS *NOW:* I climb out of the car with the intention of walking back to where she lies on the road. She's on her side with her back to me. She's a slim woman with long legs and longish brown hair that's splashed out across the blacktop. Even though I see the scratches, **EVEN** though I see the bruise on her hip, and the one on her shoulder, **EVEN** though I see she's not moving, I'm angry. I feel searing rage. I mean, my God, what a crazy thing to do! I don't give a damn about her running through the countryside, so she can expose her bare ass to the elements. But couldn't she at least ensure there's no traffic when she cavorts into a road?

The woman's maybe thirty paces from me. Still she's not moving. Now there's just a whisper of a possibility that she might be dead. What do you do with a nude corpse? How do you report such a find to the police? How do you convince them that you haven't killed her for the fun of it?

Ten paces from my car and some twenty-five from the woman my cell phone rings. That's a good reminder. Call an ambulance. This nude marathon runner isn't my responsibility.

I slip the cell phone from my belt. A glance at the screen reveals it's my business partner. No doubt he's keen for a progress report—more specifically: *Jack, do you have your hands on the film yet?*

"Not now, Steiger," I say by way of greeting. "I've just killed a woman."

"You've done what?" Steiger's normally placid tones rise in shock from the phone's speaker.

I'm still angry and continue in a no-nonsense way, "She ran out of the trees. Straight into the car. And just wait until you hear this, Steiger. She's not wearing a stitch of clothes."

"Jack, come on. You're in a bar, and you're telling me all this crap because you're stinking drunk and think it's hilarious."

"No. Steiger. Listen to me. She slammed into the car. I thought she'd come right through the windshield and into my face."

Steiger's voice rips from the speaker with enough force to make me hold the cell phone from my ear. "Don't do anything stupid, Jack. Don't hide the body. Call the police. Tell them everything. And that means the truth!"

"You think I've a reputation for lying?"

"You've a reputation for being ruthless, so don't—"

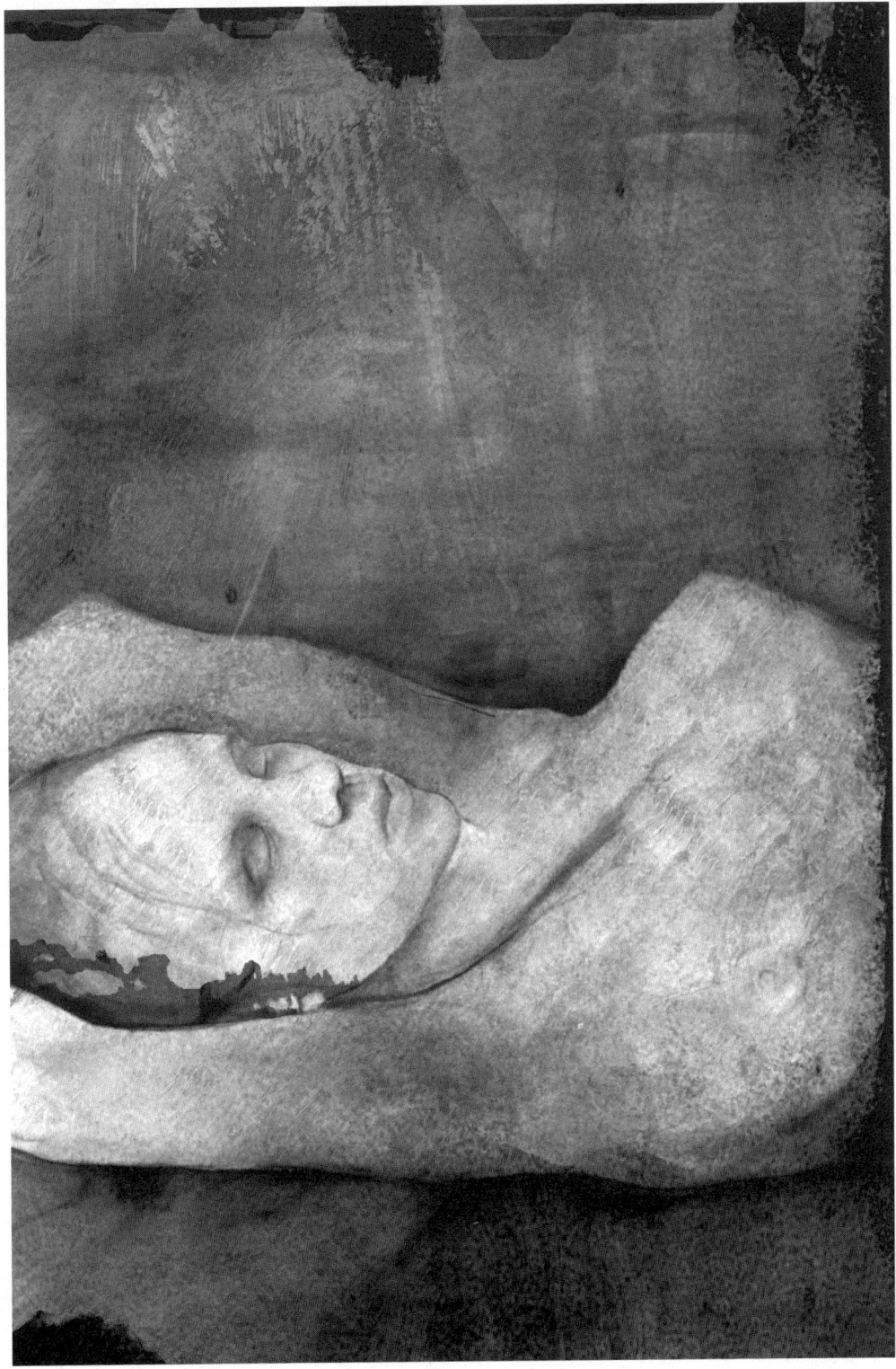

"Wait. Steiger, she's moving."

"Thank God for—"

I stop taking an interest in what Steiger's shouting from the phone as I say the first thing that comes into my head. And it's nothing to do with putting the accident victim's needs first. "What the hell were you playing at? Have you seen the damage to my car? Hey! I'm talking to you. *Hey!*"

The sun's so low that the light's in my eyes, while the woman appears to lie in a vale of shadows. She doesn't so much stand as move forward on all fours—a feline movement, a girl panther slinking away from the scene of its kill. That's the impression that darts through my head.

"*Jack? What's happening? What's she doing?*"

I don't reply as I break into a run after the woman. I don't want to console her, or ask if she's hurt. I want to give the idiot a full-blooded shaking while I yell, "You lunatic! Why the hell did you run into my car!" But like a panther she just sort of breezes away into the trees. By now she must be running on two legs rather than all fours. When I reach the section of road where her nude body had lain sprawled out with that hand-sized bruise on her hip, there's nothing much to see. I catch glimpses of her as she sprints away through the trees, her hair fluttering out. Wicked little snatches of bare buttocks, gleaming legs, lithesome torso.

"You idiot. You stupid, crazy idiot!" I roar these words after her. "Hey, listen to me. You're a lunatic. You should be locked up!"

"*Jack!*"

"You've wrecked my car! You've got to pay! Do you hear? You stupid, little—"

Panther-girl has vanished back into the wilderness. I stand there panting. I wait for a flash of naked skin to reappear.

"*Jack!*" The voice of my old friend shrills from the speaker. "*Jack! Whatever you're doing to her, stop it! Leave her alone!*"

I stand there feeling my heart thump in my chest. What a way to end a journey. Six hours of monotonous driving then this happens. Naked woman strikes car. Naked woman runs away into wilderness forest. Naked woman vanishes.

"*Jack? Jack!*"

SHE LOVES MONSTERS

At last Steiger's voice registers. I lift the cell phone to my ear. "Steiger?"

"Jack? What've you done to her?"

"I know what I'd like to do to her."

"Jack?"

"It's alright, she's run off. Listen. I'm a couple of minutes from Montage. I'll give you a call then."

"If they let you in, Jack."

"Oh, they'll let me in, all right."

"You do realize they're not going to welcome you in with open arms?"

I feel the smile on my face. "You know me, Steiger."

"Yeah, only too well, Jack."

"Speak to you later."

"Get there safely…and good hunting."

"I don't think I could catch her now."

"I'm not talking about naked strangers, Jack. You know what I mean."

"Don't hold your breath, Steiger. Treasure hunting takes time." I return the cell phone to my belt clip then walk back to the car. I'm scanning the forest all the time for the beautiful creature that made such an impression on my car's bodywork.

There's nothing. There isn't even any traffic. I haven't seen another car or truck in ten miles. After five wasted minutes of waiting for the naked runner to magically reappear I climb into the car. I find a piece of the crumpled windshield I can see through and drive in the direction of Montage, the finest piece of real estate I own. Yeah, remember to look up the word "tantalize"—and "tease" while you're at it. As a poet might say, "So near, yet *so* far away."

#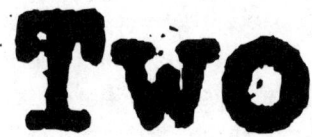

For the entire six hours of the drive to this wilderness I'd expected to be turned away. Oh yes, they were expecting me. They know who I am. They've been told Jack Calner's on the road to Montage. All the more reason, then, to lock all doors and untie the hounds.

Sure enough, there's a man waiting at the gate. This is it, I tell myself. By the hairs of his chinny-chin-chin he's not going to let me in. Only instead of turning me away the man can't wait to welcome me in. He advances through the open gates while waving me through. He's about sixty with hair that shines like chrome rather than silver. On his face, along with wire-rimmed spectacles, is the beaming smile of an avuncular monk. He doesn't appear to notice my crumpled windscreen or dented hood, or he doesn't care. Everything's nice by this man. For him the world must be an eternally happy place.

I scroll down the window with a clipped, "You know who I am?"

"Mr. Calner, yes. Miss Lake asked me to wait for you, so I can direct you to the house."

"I've just gone and found it, haven't I? Correct me if I'm wrong, but it's that geometric object with doors, windows and a dirty, great roof. Aren't I right, Jeeves?"

"Oh, my name's not Jeeves." The man's smiling so broadly I'm surprised he doesn't do himself a mischief. "I'm called Bunny."

"All butlers should be called Jeeves. It saves having to remember their names."

"I'm not a butler, Mr. Calner, I'm—"

SHE LOVES MONSTERS

"Look. I'm not interested. I've been driving all afternoon. As you can see, my car's taken a beating. I want a drink, then I have to call out a garage to replace my windshield that some lunatic tried to dive though—hey, leave the car alone, you're not going to be able to fix it. Did you hear me, buddy? Hands off."

"It's not *Buddy,* sir. My name's Bunny."

"Okay, Bunny. Take your fingers away from my car."

"But this was wrapped round the wiper, Mr. Calner."

Bunny smiles happily all through this exchange of pleasantries (and if you know me, these are pleasantries as far as I'm concerned). Now he holds out strands of hair that he's unhooked from the bent wiper.

"Uh-ho. Souvenir," I tell myself, rather than this grinning boyo. "She's left some of her mane behind." After taking the hair from him I allow the evening breeze to take the long wisps from my fingers. Strangely, the moment they float away I wish I'd held onto them. Why? I don't know. Suddenly it seems important to preserve them. Recollection of the naked woman running away into the forest still blazes bright as a chunk of the noonday sun between my ears. As I debate retrieving them the cell phone rings. My accountant. I bark into it: "Not now, Harry! Call me back in the morning." Instead of chasing through bushes in pursuit of the girl's tresses I turn my guns back onto Buddy, Bunny, Jeeves—whatever they call Mr. Happy here. He's leaning forward to smile into the car; his face is as shiny and as pink as a baby's. Must be the neighborhood idiot.

I warn him, "If you don't want me to run over your foot, keep back."

He smiles, dips his head, nodding. "Follow me up to the house, Mr. Calner."

"Follow?"

"I'll show you where to go."

"Hell. I can see the bloody house. It's right there. Fifty yards away. I'm hardly going to take a wrong turn into Death Valley, am I?"

"Miss Lake was concerned for your safety. She asked me to wait for you and guide you in."

"Dear God." I can't stop laughter bubbling out of my mouth. I do try but despite the six-hour journey, despite nearly killing a naked woman, despite Loony Tune here I've got to laugh out loud. "Guide me in! Is there some complex docking procedure when I reach the house?"

"No, sir." He chuckles happily with me. His blue eyes are alight with merry twinkles. "No docking, sir. But just behind the lilac there's a bridge over a stream and it's seen better days. If you don't drive along the main timbers your car might go through the planking."

"You are joking, aren't you?"

"Why should I tell you something that isn't true, Mr. Calner?"

"All right. I believe you, Jeeves."

"It's Bunny, sir."

"Start walking, Jeeves. I'll follow."

The man still smiles as he begins what I can tell is an important task in his mind. He's guiding me to Montage. He's going to do everything in his power to prevent my lovely, but wounded, car from falling through the bridge into the stream. He's there to keep me safe from danger. What a hero! What an adventure! I can't wait to tell Steiger about this. Once more I'm laughing as I ease the car forward in Bunny's footsteps.

But here I am at last. This is Montage. My house. My biggest asset. I want it back in my hands. And if I don't extract what I need from the parasites who live here that's exactly what I'll do.

In the growing darkness I follow the pale blob that is jolly Bunny. He makes little waving motions with one hand as I crawl the car forward. It's as if he's gently encouraging me: *Come along, Mr. Calner. Don't be frightened. Keep moving. I'll get you safely there.* The idiot. I imagine what it would be like to floor the gas pedal and allow the car to surge over him, breaking every happy bone in his body. *Will you be smiling then, Mr. Happy Bloody Bunny?*

Spanning the stream, a timber bridge that's barely longer than the car itself. The mere trickle of a brook lies about two feet beneath the timber supports. Jeeves goes to a lot of trouble to inch me across the bridge as he points to the timbers I should follow…so the car doesn't plunge through the planks. Note to self: once I reclaim possession of the house, replace bridge. Rustic stonework would be more impressive than timber.

The cell phone rings again. I check the screen as I inch the car forward over Danger Bridge (feel free to insert sarcasm icon of choice). I switch off the cell phone and lob it into the backseat. "Not tonight, Rebecca. I'm taking care of business." Then I lean out of the window to call, "Are we nearly there yet?"

SHE LOVES MONSTERS

Flashback: Being driven through this county by Dad when I'm six years old. I'm asking the man in the driving seat the same question: "Are we nearly there yet?" *And he replies:* "That we are, Jack. See the field over there? That's where I'm going to build our house. I'm going to call it Montage."

Montage—a little bit of everything. Italianate, Moorish, Gothic, English Elizabethan, American post-modern. An architectural potage.

"You built the house, Dad. But we poor schmucks never got to visit. You handed it over to your loony friend."

Smiler is now waving me forward to park on the gravel turning area at the front of the house. The only other vehicle there is a truck with the words LOCATION CATERER TO THE STARS just visible through a plague of rust on its side.

That one mile per hour creep makes my right foot ache. It's a relief to press the pedal down and roar the last few yards to park outside the front door. Bunny hurries up as I climb out of the car.

I ask him, "Where will I find Christopher Lake?"

"Oh, he'll be asleep by now, Mr. Calner."

"At eight o'clock? The sun's only just setting."

"Miss Lake asked me to show you to your room."

"Don't you mean *guide* me to my room?"

He carries on smiling like I'm the loveliest guy in the world. Not someone hell-bent on making him homeless—if I don't get what I want.

"Once you've freshened up I'll take you down to meet Miss Lake."

I grunt. "I'll be able to find the lounge by myself. Unless there are any dangerous bridges indoors to cross?"

"No, nothing like that, sir. But it is a big house."

"Glad to hear it. At least my father did one thing right."

"Sir?"

"Never mind. Lead on, Jeeves."

"My name's Bunny, sir."

And after all my sulphuric comments the man's still smiling.

"Just show me my room." I pull my weekend bag from the backseat. When I see the depression in the hood created by the woman's naked body impacting the car it's enough to send the blood blazing through my veins. "Find me a glass on the way. I've a very nice single malt. I don't plan drinking something as expensive as that from the bottle."

Three

Bunny takes me to the guest room. It lies beneath the dome in one corner of the house. He never stops smiling. Bunny's either the happiest man in the world, or his doctor needs to prescribe something a little less powerful. I mean, surely this guy has to be gorging on some powerful pharmaceuticals to make him so unrelentingly cheerful. At the door of the room I glance back as he stands at the top of the stairs. With the electric light shining on that abundantly silver hair of his he appears more like a saint than a genial monk now. If wincingly cute little bluebirds alighted on his arms I shouldn't have been in the least surprised.

"Everything you need is in your room, Mr. Calner."

"I doubt everything," I tell him as I step inside. "Be back here at nine on the nail. I'll see Miss Lake then."

He utters words I don't catch as I shut the door in that genial face. The dent in my car still infuriates me. So, first things first, I pull the whisky from my bag then pour a meaty slug into the glass on the bedside table. Once I've rolled a mouthful of that wonderful single malt across my tongue and swallowed with a grateful sigh, then I take more notice of my room here in Montage. As I said, it's under the bronze dome that thrusts up with phallic splendor from the corner of the house. *Dad, I've got to ask, did you ever read Freud?* The ceiling echoes the curve to create a rising vault above my head. The room is richly furnished. There's a large bed with an ornate iron frame that sports finials that resemble lotus flowers. Beneath my feet there's what could be an antique Persian rug. Before I leave I'll make an inventory of the fur-

SHE LOVES MONSTERS

nishings; I probably inherited them all with the house. The walls are painted sunflower yellow and the lantern hanging down from the convex ceiling is a Moorish style lamp in polished brass.

I check the bathroom. Dated, but it'll banish road dust.

Another swallow of whisky and I take a look out through the window. It's nearly dark now. I don't see any lights from other houses. An absence that suggest there are no neighbors for miles. What I can see of the road is deserted. This is the ideal rustic retreat. What sticks in my throat is that it's become a lunatic asylum for one. A solitary madman. Dad left me holding the baby. That's the phrase that lingers irritatingly in my head.

I gaze up at the ceiling as I raise the glass of malt in a toast. "I'm here, Dad. I've made it to Montage. Cheers." I take a deeply satisfying swallow. Those Scots got something right when they called their liquor "the water of life." It energizes. I smile at my reflection in the wall mirror. I've got the same shaped eyes as my late departed, gone to the hereafter, father. But they're not soft like his. They're hard. Hard as tungsten. And I tell you now that is a feature I'm proud of. If Dad's loopy friends don't cooperate they're going to learn the hard way that, for once, the maxim "like father like son" won't run true.

Four

After a brisk shower I dress for power, not for comfort. A charcoal Armani suit, white shirt, a narrow necktie in dark blue. Shoes are important. From my bag I extract black leather brogues that have been buffed until they shine like gunmetal. Bunny knows the meaning of punctuality. On the stroke of nine he escorts me downstairs to meet Miss Lake in a lounge that's cavernous enough to double as a Zeppelin hangar. This room is in the classical Greek style with marble columns and statues of gods and heroes armed with spears. They stand along the walls, guarding Montage against intruders like me. There are huge ferns sprouting from amphorae. On the ceiling a painted Zeus is hurling lightning bolts across a turbulent sky. Enemies are well and truly smited. The place smells of garlic. I hate garlic.

"Mr. Calner," Bunny intones with a beatific smile, "Miss Lake won't be but a moment."

"I'd rather hoped she'd be here to meet me. This isn't a social call."

Bunny doesn't so much walk out of the room as withdraw backward from it with a smile and a slow bobbing of the head. It irritates me that the Lake woman isn't here waiting; however, it gives me a chance to examine the statues. They've got to be copies; nevertheless, they'll still be valuable. By the French doors is a naked goddess with an ass that is nothing less than Olympian. Now, there's a rear that should be the Eighth Wonder of the World. With a smile I move on. I'm examining the carving of Apollo, standing with his chin up, adopting a noble stance in his warrior's helmet, when I hear footsteps on the mosaic floor.

"Mr. Calner."

SHE LOVES MONSTERS

I turn to see a woman…no, a girl. She approaches me with all the confidence of a fawn approaching a grizzly bear. She's slim with dark hair tied back into a ponytail. An orange flower is pinned above her left ear. Her eyes are brown and so large that they accentuate the thin face—the kind of face some fanciful people might describe as elfin. She's made an effort to be decorous even though she's not displaying any jewelry, whatsoever. She's wearing a bright turquoise dress with electric blue swirls. It reaches below her knees and buttons halfway up her neck. Women calibrate their fashions with their peers. This woman—this girl—clearly has no peers. She lives out here in the wilderness and copies fashion designs from magazines that have been lying under a sofa for decades.

Anyway, to cut away the fudge of superfluous descriptions: here is a shy girl with an apprehensive smile dressed in peculiar hippy fabrics. I can't wait to see Mr. Lake, if the daughter's anything to go by.

"Mr. Calner?" she repeats.

"Yes."

"Hello. I'm Venus Lake."

"Venus?" I frown. "You're not Christopher Lake's sister?"

She smiles nervously. "Yes, I am."

"You're younger than I expected."

"Thank you."

"It wasn't intended to be a compliment." I mentally review my facts. "According to my father's papers you're thirty-seven."

"That's right. Oh, I'm sorry to hear about your loss, Mr. Calner. Jeremy was such a nice man."

"Yes. He was *nice,* wasn't he?" I can't help rendering the word "nice" as if it's as derogatory as the descriptions "soft" or "meek." Dad was an easy touch. I'm standing in the proof right now.

"Your father loved to drive here through the mountains. He called them the Aspirin Hills, because every time he saw them his headache would disappear."

"Really."

"What he liked best was to help Bunny in the garden. They'd mow the lawns and tidy the flowerbeds. The last time he was here he sketched out a bridge to replace the old one. He said it would be our Japanese bridge like you'd find—"

"Miss Lake. I stated in my letter this wouldn't be a social call."

She gives one of those awkward, shy smiles that weak people favor. "Sorry. Yes. You wanted to discuss my brother's work."

"And the house. I inherited Montage from my father. The production company passed to me, too. What there is of it."

"I hope you're going to start making films again. The last film of your father's was beautiful. I'm hoping I can afford a player so I...oh, please sit down." She perches on the edge of a sofa. If anything she appears even more nervous.

I remain standing. "I've been driving the best part of the day, so being on my feet's preferable. Now, to get to the point, I've a lot to do this weekend."

"Of course, I apologize for...you know...we don't get many visitors."

"You do understand why I'm here, Miss Lake?"

"Yes...well, I think so."

"My father's records show there are two people living here. Yourself and your brother, Christopher Lake."

"That's right."

"And the man who calls himself Bunny?"

"He lives in the summer house in the garden...it's not really a summer house, more of a cottage. There's electricity and—"

"Does he pay you rent?"

"No. He helps out here. I don't know what we'd do without him."

I click my tongue. "There's no record of him signing a tenancy agreement."

"Oh, that's okay. Your father knew all about Bunny. He said it was all right for him to live in the summer house."

"Miss Lake, it's not all right. If he's not signed a tenancy agreement then he might claim squatter's rights, which hampers my right to do what I wish with my property."

This makes her flinch. She's maybe had a sneak preview of her future. "Mr. Calner, your father promised we could stay here."

"My father is dead, Miss Lake. Regrettable though that loss is for both you and myself, the fact remains that ownership of Montage has passed to me. It's customary for a tenant to pay rent on a property they occupy. I know for a fact you never paid a penny in rent to my father...nor to me."

SHE LOVES MONSTERS

"I'm sorry." Flustered, she's more apologetic than defensive. "My brother had an agreement with your father. They decided that they would have equal shares in the profits of the films. In return my brother would live here."

I sigh. "But that never happened, did it?" With that I sit in the large armchair that faces her. I draw a cigar from my pocket. Her eyes follow me with all the concentration of someone watching a surgical procedure as I use my gold cutters to amputate the sealed tip of the cigar. Maybe she doesn't want me to smoke. Oh dear…oh dear, oh dear, oh dear… My house, missy.

To smoke in someone else's home is to stake a possessory claim. Just like a male dog cocking its leg to piss against a tree. The symbolism isn't lost on her.

I lock eye contact on her. For a moment I say nothing. I'm demonstrating I dictate the pace of this meeting. Then: "Miss Lake. Listen carefully. I'm a businessman. I take my money and my property seriously."

"Your father was very proud of you. He liked to—"

I talk over her. "I'm going to tell you what I've been able to learn from the office files about my father's business relationship with your brother. When I've finished, add any facts I might have missed. Correct any misapprehensions. Then I'll make a financial proposition that your brother will have to agree to in a written contract."

"That won't be possible."

"There's no *possibles* or *maybes* or *equivocation* whatsoever, Miss Lake," I tell her. "Come what may, I'll be leaving here tomorrow with Mr. Lake's signature on that document."

"I'm really sorry, Mr. Calner." Her brown eyes are big and frightened. "It's impossible."

"Believe me…in this matter, you don't have the right to say what is or is not impossible. Do you understand?"

"I understand. And I am sorry." Tears aren't far away. "But before you get angry with me, Mr. Calner, I'd like you to come with me and see my brother."

Five

So I follow her upstairs. It's now so dark that she has to switch on the lights in each section of corridor in this sprawling house. It's completely silent. The smell reminds me of a museum; the trigger is that evocative odor of old wood and floor polish, maybe a subtler whiff of lives frozen in time, too. When she reaches a door at the end of the corridor she gently taps on the panel.

"Christopher? It's only me."

She opens the door in that tentative way of hers, as if afraid of what she'll find on the other side. I follow her into a room that's as sparsely furnished as a hermit's cell. Perhaps the only concession to the modern world is a laptop standing on a bedside table. The moment she switches on the light I see a bed with a bearded guy stretched out on in it. With the beard and long hair he resembles one of those old portrayals of Jesus. His brown eyes are open. They stare at the ceiling.

He's dead, I tell myself in surprise. He's stone dead. She's left him here to rot. I picture a million squirming maggots. Only no sooner does the thought go skipping through my head than he comes to life. He sits up in bed and begins to pull off his T-shirt.

"No, Christopher." Her voice is gentle. "It's not time to get up yet."

There's no emotion on his face. He doesn't acknowledge our presence. He just stares at the wall as if he can see through it into the distance. The guy's clean. Well-nourished without being fat. The nails on his hands are evenly shaped as if they've been manicured. The man, however, is clearly absent from reality. He tries to climb out of bed again with a mechanical slowness. There's no spark there; it's merely an automatic process.

SHE LOVES MONSTERS

"Christopher." His sister puts her hand on his shoulder to signal to him that he should remain there. "It's not morning yet. Stay in bed."

He regards her with dead eyes.

"Christopher. This is Mr. Calner. He's Jeremy's son." No response. The zombie expression doesn't even flicker. "Look. Christopher...*look.*" It's like trying to show a baby a visitor. "Look, this is Jeremy's son. He's come to see you." She makes waggling movements with her fingers in front of his face. When his eyes at last lock onto the fingers she moves her hand so as to draw his captured gaze to my face. "This is Jack Calner... You remember Jeremy talking about his son? Jeremy showed you a photograph of the graduation. Remember the cap and gown?"

For a second the man's dead eyes rest on my face. They don't focus, they simply happen to gaze in my direction.

"Put your T-shirt back on, Christopher. That's it." She helps him with it. "Go back to sleep now." She has the soothing voice of a mother settling a child. "Make yourself comfortable. There, let your head rest back on the pillow."

He obeys in that mechanical way. A moment later his eyes stare up at the ceiling.

"See, Mr. Calner? My brother isn't capable of signing any documents."

"He's always like this?"

She nods.

I click my tongue. "For how long?"

"Twelve years this July."

"I'd been told that Mr. Lake had become a recluse after his breakdown. I didn't expect this." I turn to the thing on the bed that my father once described as a genius. "Mr. Lake. Do you know where you are?"

Lake doesn't respond. He lies on his back as he gazes at the ceiling with that blank, zombie expression.

This is a setback, I tell myself. This is a problem. Thank God, I'm one of those men who feed on problems. Conflict fires me into overdrive. Good! Make this treasure hunt difficult. It'll prompt me to perform even better. Obstacles—not an easy ride—are the real keys to success.

"Miss Lake. A moment ago I said I'd outline what I know about my father's contract with your brother here. Tell me if I've got this right. Your brother was a filmmaker. In his early twenties he produced three feature films that are now considered by people who like that kind of thing as classics." Crisply, I reel off the titles. *"Triangle, Octagon* and *Ellipse."* Venus Lake appears daunted by my knowledge of her brother. She nods in that timid way of hers while I continue without hesitation. "Together they sell a million copies a year in DVD. The commercial rights to the stills alone turn over five million a year. I'm correct, aren't I?"

She nods. "But we don't make any money from them. Nothing."

"I know. You were stitched up by the studio's contract. Your brother made the films for a flat fee without securing a share in either gross or net profits." I move swiftly on. "Then fifteen years ago enter my father, Jeremy Calner. He agrees to finance Christopher's fourth film. I was fourteen years old at the time. I remember him being very excited about the deal. The money meant nothing in his eyes. All that interested him was that he'd be working with a filmmaker who critics described as the new Orson Welles."

"But he wasn't—"

"No, Christopher Lake wasn't a new Welles. My father told me he was a Lon Chaney, HP Lovecraft and Tod Browning rolled into one. The names meant nothing to me until I researched them a few days ago. Whether or not those individuals were geniuses or charlatans I don't know, but I do know they are marketable. So my father funded your brother's fourth and final film, a production entitled *Vorada*. And subtitled: *I Am Your Death*. He began it fifteen years ago. Thirteen years ago he screened portions of it to a private audience. Then with my father's consent Lake moved here to Montage to complete it. As I say, that was thirteen years ago. I'm entitled to fifty percent of *Vorada's* gross profits. And so here's my question to you: Where is the film?"

"I'm sorry, Mr. Calner, I don't know."

"Don't know? Or won't say?"

"I've not seen the reels in ten years."

I turn to the man in bed. "Mr. Lake. Where's the film? Where do you keep it?" No response. *"Vorada.* Come on, you must know where it is?"

Venus Lake is frightened but she forces herself to speak. "Mr.

SHE LOVES MONSTERS

Calner. Please don't try and talk to Christopher. He doesn't speak to anyone. He hasn't for years."

"What's wrong with him?"

"He went into a decline when he was making the film. He'd nearly finished it when he suffered a breakdown. He'd exhausted himself making it."

"But he screened some excerpts? My father saw part of it."

"Yes, but Christopher became very anxious about the film."

"Anxious? Why?"

"I don't know. When he came back here after showing parts of the film he continued work in the editing suite, but he wouldn't let anyone see it. He even locked himself in the room with it. When I asked if I could see it he refused; he said the film wasn't right."

"Those exact words? 'The film wasn't right?' "

"Yes."

"What did he mean by that?"

"I don't know."

"Come on, Miss Lake, you must realize what your brother was implying. 'The film's not right.' That means it's not finished, or not good enough. Or 'not right' in a moral sense?"

She shrugs.

I press the point home. "After all, 'the film's not right,' could mean that it might be condemned as being sadistic or pornographic, or even downright evil."

Venus Lake doesn't answer.

I push the interrogation. "So, the situation is this: your brother had finished the film in an editing suite here in the house. Other than a few clips at a private screening it's never been seen in its entirety. Your brother told you 'the film wasn't right.' Then the reels vanished?"

She nods.

"And your brother became a recluse here and suffered a mental deterioration to the point we see him today. Uncommunicative to say the least."

She gives that pained nod again.

"Good." I smile. "It makes the hunt interesting, anyway."

"I'm sorry, Mr. Calner. I don't know if the film exists anymore. He might have destroyed it."

"The bottom line is this," I tell her. "Either I find *Vorada,* which as you know will be worth millions to both of us. Or I'll consider your brother's contract with my father void. In that case, I'll require you to move out of Montage within twenty-eight days." My smile broadens at her wide-eyed expression. "That's right, Miss Lake, the truth is finally sinking in. I either drive away tomorrow with the film—or I'll have my house back. Thank you very much."

Six

The pounding on the door brings me out of bed before I'm fully awake. I'm cursing because I can't find a light switch in the unfamiliar room, but I do find the door handle and wrench it open in a rage.

Venus Lake is standing there in white cotton pajamas that simper innocence and beauty. *"Help me!"*

She's barely got the words through her lips when she turns and runs along the corridor. I go after the woman, wondering what fun and games she's got planned for this time of night. As I follow her mad dash downstairs she cries out to me, "It's Christopher. He's set fire to the house!"

God Almighty. The one-time genius is crazier than I gave him credit for. "Venus!" I drop the Miss Lake in view that it's *my* house burning down. "Venus, where's your fire extinguisher?"

"There isn't one."

She disappears into the living room. When I smell acrid smoke I move faster.

And when I enter the living room with its statues and mosaic floor this is what I see: Christopher Lake is sitting in an armchair. And that armchair isn't just alight, it's spewing flames. I mean jets of flame like it's been hit by napalm. The lights aren't on but the fire is so brilliant I have to shield my eyes as I run forward. Venus is screaming at her brother to get out of the burning chair. But all he does is sit there. His forearms are supported by the arm rest. Same zombie expression on his face. The dull eyes stare into the distance. I lunge at the madman. Now that I'm closer I see he's wearing a leather flying jacket. Other than the chair blazing to high heaven he could be some idle schmuck lazing in front of the TV.

"**MOVE!**" I don't wait for him to obey. I grab him by the front of the jacket and lift him out of the chair like he's a rag doll and throw him away from the flames. I see him go tumbling across the mosaic floor.

"Venus! Open the French windows." I'm gambling the doors I've ordered her to open do exit outside. It's too late now. I've got to go for it. The flames are bursting from the sides of the chair. The headrest is still untouched, so this is the part I grab to start pushing the chair across the floor on its castors. Within seconds I'm running with this chair that's rapidly becoming a ball of fire. I feel my face smart from the heat of it. The black smoke shrouds me. It's in my eyes and throat. The fumes reach my lungs. It hurts so much it's like rats gnawing inside of me. A hundred sharp teeth crunching through lung tissue.

I yell at her, "Get out of my way!" I see enough of the open doorway to charge through, shoving the burning chair in front of me. Then I'm outside, gulping down cold night air. Finally, I kick the armchair across the patio, so it's well away from the house. There it burns like a torch, like a great fucking torch. The kind you see in medieval castles. It spits burning plastic onto the stone slabs. The flames are a tower of light jetting into the night sky.

I turn away from it. My eyes are streaming, I'm coughing. By the time I get back indoors I'm roaring at the man lying there on the mosaic floor of dolphins and fish swimming through a surreal ocean.

"You idiot...you crazy bastard! You could have burned the house down! You nearly killed us!" I glare at the man who reclines there like a child who is mildly surprised by nothing more than a window banging in the wind. Venus is crouching beside him. She examines his hands, no doubt checking to see if he's burnt his mindless, arsonist self. I continue my rant, "You should be in the nut house. Do you hear me? You should be locked away!"

"I'm sorry," gulps his sister. "He's never done anything like this before. I don't know...he's...I'm sorry. Look... Please don't hurt him." She's so shocked she hardly knows what she's saying. She examines him in a trembling way, her hands shaking.

I take a breath. My heart's still pounding. Adrenaline's taking me on a real rush. A sky-high, nerve-spangling rush-a-roo. Even so, my voice is coming down a notch or two. "Is he hurt?"

"The jacket protected him. It's scorched but he seems okay."

"Okay? Venus, for a pyromaniac he's as okay as he will ever be."

"I don't understand." Then she repeats the statement: "He's never done anything like this before."

"You mean he's never tried to burn the house down?"

"I haven't even seen him strike a match in ten years." She's aghast. For a moment she dips her head in defeat. She's shaking her head and her long brown hair tumbles forward. The pajama top is loose around the collar. Part of it slips off her shoulder. A bright red scratch in her skin runs from the back of her neck to end in a whopping purple bruise on her shoulder. She senses I'm looking at her. Quickly she stands upright while adjusting the neckline of the pajama top to cover the injury. She pulls her long brown hair down over her neck to hide the scratch, too. For an instant her big, dark eyes flick up onto mine, then glance away—that frightened deer look again.

Forcing herself to speak, she asks, "Are you alright?"

"Never better." I flex my right fist. A tightness in my fingers tells me I've scorched them.

"You've burnt your hand."

"Lightly toasted. It's nothing."

Venus finds it hard to look me in the eye. "I'll find you some antiseptic for it."

"It'll be fine." But she disappears so quickly it's as if she's flitted away like a bird. I go to check on the burning armchair. "That better not be valuable," I say aloud as I look out through the doorway. There it is: a sad skeleton of burning wood. One thing's for sure, it's not going to damage anything now that it's isolated from the house. It can burn itself out on the patio.

When I hear a footstep I turn around. "Venus?" Instead of the woman it's brother Christopher who stands behind me. The leather flying jacket is burnt black in parts but it clearly saved the lunatic's bacon. I tell him, "You might as well enjoy what's left of your pyrotechnics. Just promise me you won't try setting fire to my house again?"

He gazes at the burning bones of the chair. His face is lit by the yellow flame. It's reflected in his wide staring eyes. Then suddenly they narrow as if for the first time in years thought has entered that hollow head of his.

His lips part, his teeth catch the firelight in golden glints. There's an inward rush of air through his mouth. With the exhalation a second later come words. They're whispered. So quiet I have to strain to hear them.

"Find my film," he tells me as he stares at the burning chair. "She took it from me. Destroy it before she can use it."

Seven

Venus is back with the salve before I can question the man further. Christopher Lake, meanwhile, retreats into himself. Staring vacantly with that zombied look again, he utters zilch. He does nothing but stand there and gaze at the remains of the burning furniture.

"Mr. Calner? I have the cream. I'll put some on for you." After switching on the table lamp she sits on the sofa. I go sit beside her. I'm still shooting glances at Christopher. His words have taken me by surprise. *Find my film. She took it from me. Destroy it before she can use it.* How does that equate with one of his last cogent statements ten years ago that Venus repeated to me: *The film wasn't right.* Question mark? Not just any question mark. This is a huge symbol of the mystery that punctuates the atmosphere in this mausoleum of a house.

I'm sure Venus hasn't heard Lake's plea to me, so for the time being I decide to say nothing about it. Now she's squeezing antiseptic cream from the tube onto the tip of her slim finger. A clock on the mantelpiece chimes 2 a.m.

As I sit beside her she takes my hand, rests it on her pajama clad lap and gently begins to smooth the cream into my scorched skin. Her fingers are cooler than the salve and the movements gentle as she can make. Christopher still stares out at the burning ruin of the chair.

"I've been thinking," she says. "We can start looking for the film in the editing suite. There are more cans of film in the garage as well." She applies another blob of cream to my reddened knuckles. "As far as I know, Christopher had finished shooting all the material he needed for the film. And he'd decided on the title. *Vorada.* I'm sorry." Venus

SHE LOVES MONSTERS

flinches because she's found the burn has raised a blister on my little finger. "I didn't mean to hurt you." As if handling a live butterfly she carefully dabs more of the salve onto the blister. "There's local anesthetic in the ointment. It should stop hurting soon." Then she returns to the subject of the film. "The first cut of *Vorada* ran to eight hours. I know Christopher spent months in the editing suite to bring it down to four hours. Then he became ill..." The memory pains her, though she forces a tiny smile on to her face that suddenly has a fairy tale beauty in this muted light. "It was his mind. He'd worked too hard on the film. Chrissie started hiding himself away in the garden...behind walls or lying under bushes. There's even a cave in the grotto where he..." She bites her lip. "Anyway. He finished work on the film. Then he just stopped functioning. He hasn't talked for years. Not a word." She turns her face to me, meeting my eyes for the first time that evening in a long unblinking look. "How long do you plan to stay?"

My eyes fix on hers, holding the gaze. "Venus? Why did you run out in front of my car today?"

She shakes her head, then whispers a very tight-lipped, "No."

"So how did you get the bruise on your shoulder—and the scratch on your neck?"

Again that shake of the head. She looks away from me as if in shame.

I raise my voice. "Or did your brother use you as a punching bag?"

She whirls away from the sofa. A second later she's rushing away in the direction of the hallway door.

"*Venus! Why did you run into the front of the car? Why were you naked?*"

Eight

The instant I wake up I make a decision. I want Venus Lake. And I don't intend to wait long. For a moment I sit on the edge of the bed beneath that bronze domed ceiling, the birds are making a racket outside, the breeze is blowing scents of a countryside in Spring through the windows. It's not a pretty perfume of fruit blossom, it's that prickling odor of stinging nettles; with that is an underlying mustiness of wild hemlock.

I'm drawing in that smell and I'm thinking where I'd like to touch Venus Lake. Her of the slender waist and large brown eyes that are so soulful. Frankly it surprises me that I'm taken with the woman. She's timid, she's nothing more than a full-time nurse to an empty pot of a brother. Maybe it's the challenge? She seems beyond the range of many a man's hunting prowess. It's that old case of *because I can't have that's exactly what I want.* I WANT Venus Lake. And I repeat to myself under my breath it's only lust, not love. Love's a treacherous and unpredictable force.

There's also another element to the attraction.

I murmur the words for the pleasure of saying this revelation out loud: "Venus Lake runs through the woods naked." I know she's the individual who crashed across the hood of my car yesterday and shattered the windshield. Last night I saw the scratches and bruising. With her brown hair loose around her shoulders it made her resemble the naked figure I saw in the gloom. It's strange to say, but I'm impressed the way she bounced off half a ton of German steelwork then seconds later raced away into the trees like a panther. It's as if being knocked down hardly fazed her. "Intriguing."

SHE LOVES MONSTERS

Briskly, I shower, treat myself to the closest of shaves, then dress in an open necked lemon-colored shirt and chinos. After the businessman's uniform of last night I can afford to dress down for the treasure hunt today. Especially now I know Venus can do nothing to prevent me from searching for the lost *Vorada*. I'm not interested in the film's story line. Go on, strike me down, but I haven't even bothered to ask what it's about. What's important to me is that the theatrical, DVD and stills rights will form a constructive arc of my investment portfolio (as will this house before very long). That's what I find compelling—not screenplays, nor actors' performances and all the precious activity that goes with movie making. When I get my hands on the film reels I'll be calculating *Vorada's* ability to generate revenue. Dollars, pounds sterling, euros, yen, pesos. You can disregard art, religion, science…and you can even turn your nose up at politics. The truth is, my friend, money is the engine that powers the world.

It's six-thirty. The early sunlight slices through the windows in dazzling rods of gold. There's no one about. All I can hear is birdsong. My view consists of garden, meadows, woodland and hills.

My thoughts are drawn back to Venus Lake. After I identified Venus as the woman who'd bounced merrily off my car yesterday she didn't admit or deny it, she simply rushed from the room. No matter. That's a minor issue that can be cleared up later. Along with another issue of peeling away the rest of her defensive layers. The thought produces a tingle in my scalp.

I hum softly to myself as I go downstairs to find the kitchen. At least the Lakes don't dine exclusively on cracked nuts and fruit. I find coffee and cereals. That's ample breakfast for me. After I've eaten I take a walk. Now, at last, I can take a good look at Montage in the daylight. First of all, of course, I pass the film caterer's truck that's clearly reached the end of its useful life. And then my car that still bears signs of the impact of Venus's naked body.

As for Montage, I get to appreciate its mix of architectural styles properly for the first time. Some windows are oblong, some narrowing at the top into pointed arches in a Moorish style. A couple of the walls are bare stone while the rest are rendered either in pale green or yellow. The property is enclosed by post and rail fencing. Beyond that are fields that roll away to forests and hills. As I walk I flex the hand that suffered a lick of flame from the burning chair. Apart from one small blister on my little finger there's no damage to speak of. At the back of the house I cross the patio with a small mound of ash upon it. It's all that remains of Christopher Lake's act of pyromania.

In the sun slanting through trees I see a figure standing at a pair of double gates set in a garden wall. He's tugging at them without much success.

I stroll across to him. "Having trouble getting in, Bunny?"

Bunny casts a benevolent smile back over his shoulder at me; his spectacles catch the sunlight in peculiar little heliograph flashes as if he's signaling a concealed message. "Good morning, Mr. Calner." He tugs at the gates again. They are heavy duty things in wrought iron. They wouldn't look out of place in a prison.

"What do you keep on the other side of the gates, Bunny? Gold bullion?"

"Mr. Lake was very interested in keeping the barn secure."

"Barn?" I step up to the gates to look through the bars. Beyond a stretch of lush stinging nettles that occupies the intervening space like a green pond I see a single story timber building with a red tiled roof. "What's the fascination with that? It's derelict."

"Oh, it's in fair order, sir." Bunny has no luck opening the gates, but it doesn't stop him tugging at them. The hinges are rusted solid. "It just hasn't been used in a while."

"A long while, it looks to me. Here, you take the left hand one. No, stand further to the left so I can get hold." We stand side-by-side as we grip the vertical bars. "Okay, Bunny. On the count of three, pull. And I mean really pull. Don't just play at it. One, two, three."

We both tug hard. Bunny's no muscleman but he gives it everything he's got. With a piercing scream the gate judders open.

"Now for the next one." We do the same. It opens as if begrudging the favor. A scream of iron. Flakes of rust cascade from the hinges. "If I were you," I pant, "I'd oil them from time to time." Now we're faced with that barrier of stinging nettles that are as high as my chest. It's probably these venomous beauties that I smelt in my bedroom. "Well, that's the gates open. But you're going to give yourself some pain walking through those nettles."

Bunny smiles. "And there's brambles grown up over the door as well. I'll cut them down with a scythe."

SHE LOVES MONSTERS

I brush the rust off my palms. "It passes the time, I suppose."

Bunny shakes his head. "Miss Lake asked me to clear a way to the door for you."

"For me?"

"In there." He points at the barn as he walks away. "It's Mr. Lake's place where he worked on his films."

"It's the editing suite?"

He nods his gray head. "Miss Lake says you need to look inside."

"Bring another scythe, Bunny. I'll give you a hand." Now I'm keen to see what's in there. I'd joked about the gold bullion, but if *Vorada* is beyond those nettles then that ramshackle building might as well be Aladdin's cave.

In a minute he's back with a couple of scythes with handles that are as long as I am tall. Soon we're working side-by-side, slicing through lush nettle stalks that leave a smear of green juice on the blades. We make good progress through the swath of plants that extends twenty feet or so to the entrance of what served as Lake's editing suite. By this time I'm aware that Venus Lake stands on the patio watching us work. When we reach the door and cut down the last of the nettles and briars that bar our way to what I hope is the treasure house, the woman walks down the lawn to the gate. She wears a purple skirt that reaches her calves. With that, a white blouse. This morning I find myself noticing the curves of her body and the texture of the smooth skin on her face. Longing becomes an ache that creeps into my body. Good Lord, I didn't plan this. I find myself smiling.

"Good morning," I say brightly.

She nods. I sense a wariness. "Good morning, Jack. Did you sleep well?"

"Perfectly." She calls me by my first name. Before it was Mr. Calner, never Jack. Maybe when we saved the house from burning down last night we both crossed some kind of threshold. Partners in the face of adversity—that kind of thing.

"I've brought you the key to the barn." She holds it up as she steps forward.

I shout at her: *"No!"* She stops with a startled expression on her face. "You're wearing sandals," I explain. "We've chopped down the nettles but they're still ankle deep. You'll get stung if you try walking across."

"Oh."

I lean the scythe against the wall. "Stay there. I'll carry you across."

Will she permit me getting that close? For a moment I imagine her running away from me and back to the house.

Venus is pliant. She allows me to pick her up. Then, like a new husband carrying his fresh bride over the threshold of their home, I lift her with one arm under her spine and one under the backs of her thighs.

Shyly, she looks down so she doesn't have to make eye contact as I bear her across the rug of fallen nettles to the door. She hands Bunny the door key. He has to wrestle with the padlock for a moment before he can unfasten it. It gives me plenty of time to hold her. She's as light as air in my arms. A faint, pleasant scent rises from her body. I can feel her bones through her skin and clothes.

"There you go, Mr. Calner." Bunny pushes the door open. Again old hinges squeal like they resent being woken from a deep slumber. Into the dusty interior I carry the woman who I intend to hold again very soon.

"This is an editing suite?" I look round. "It'd pass for a junk yard."

I set Venus down on her sandaled feet as she gazes round the chaotic interior. "Before Christopher's big breakdown he became very disorganized."

"Is this the viewer?" I touch a contraption that's the size of a refrigerator with a TV size screen on top and a pair of spindles where I suspect the spools are placed.

"It's the editing machine," she explains. "These hinged metal plates are the splicer. It's used to cut the celluloid and re-attach the ends. You can still see drops of glue on the bench that Christopher used to splice it together."

"Is this part of the film?" I point to a rack against one wall from where strips of celluloid hang down in brown strands.

"They're outtakes from his earlier work, not *Vorada*."

"How do you know?"

"He was most particular about that film, Jack. He never left so much as a frame of *Vorada* out on show. When he wasn't working on it he kept it in the safe up at the house."

"So we're not going to find the film here?"

In the gloom her eyes are large glittery orbs as she shakes her head.

"Then why allow Bunny and me to go to all the trouble of clearing the way to the editing suite?"

"You'd have wanted to check here for yourself."

"So, next stop the safe?"

"If you like. It's empty."

"Okay." I give a philosophical shrug. "We search the house. Any ideas where to start?"

"As I told you yesterday, Jack, I haven't seen the film cans for years. It's likely my brother destroyed them."

"Like he nearly burnt the house down last night."

She assents with a shrug.

"So why do you run naked through the woods?"

Her frowning glance at me reveals that she hoped I wouldn't be so impolite as to raise the bare marathon stuff again.

"I'll go back to the house and start lunch." She makes a decision. "I'll tell you then."

With that she turns and runs through the cropped nettles. The sandals are secured to her bare feet by the thinnest of straps. Her nude toes, feet and ankles must be badly stung by the venomous plants but she gives no indication of noticing the pain.

Why do I find myself thinking that Montage is a house full of secrets that are just itching to break out? A vessel full to the gunnels with mystery? A building awash with skewed perspectives? Forgive my purple prose. But this is just the kind of place that provokes melodramatic notions. Strange house. Strange, *strange* inhabitants.

Bunny smiles from outside the doorway as he wipes away the nettle's poisonous juices from the scythe with a rag. "You'll like Miss Lake's cooking."

I tell him straight, "That's not all of hers I'm going to enjoy."

The monk-like Bunny continues smiling at me. I can't see his eyes behind his spectacles. Instead I see an image of myself reflected in the lenses. I notice an expression of yearning in my face. I want Venus Lake. I know I've got it bad. That surprises me. But it's not a problem. Everything that life tosses in your direction you can turn to your advantage. Learn to do that, and the rewards are there for your taking. Fail...and you're doomed to a life of hell on earth.

Nine

A sense of tantalizing promise hangs in the air. Not simply the search for *Vorada* or Venus's impending elaboration on her nude roving across the countryside, but I have that taste in my mouth. You know the one. The taste you get when you're close to breaking through someone's defenses, and either clinching a business deal or taking a woman in her bed. And that taste, my friend, is the taste of conquest.

Before lunch I've time to telephone the only garage in forty miles. With it being Saturday morning they can't replace the windshield until Monday. So I'm here for an extra couple of nights. That's no hardship. Something tells me there'll be entertainment aplenty here. I make calls to my business partner and accountant. I postpone a Monday morning meeting until Tuesday. I have to tell them that I haven't got my hands on *Vorada* yet, Mr. Lake's famous lost film for which critics and fans alike have been baying non-stop over the last decade. But I'm close. I'm very close. Here's what I've figured out so far: Lake is mentally ill. He'd been insanely possessive of the film, so he wouldn't have destroyed it. Also, remember his words from last night. Seeing as he hadn't spoken in years, his plea: *"Find my film. She took it from me. Destroy it before she can use it"* was potent indeed. This is where the proverbial slack-faced dummy asks, "What's all that about then?" But the mentally dissipated Christopher Lake's three sentences are lucid enough to me.

First sentence: *Find my film.* If Lake wants me to find the film—undoubtedly *Vorada*—then the film is capable of being found; therefore, it still exists.

SHE LOVES MONSTERS

Second sentence: *She took it from me.* The only "she" for miles around is the man's sister, Venus Lake. He believes Venus seized possession of the film reels. That means, despite her pretense at ignorance, she knows full well the whereabouts of the missing "masterpiece."

Third sentence, a most mysterious and provocative sentence: *Destroy it before she can use it.* What does one infer from that? That not only is the content of the film dangerous in some way, but Christopher Lake is terrified that his sister will "use" the film. For commercial gain? To expose a dangerous secret? As a weapon? This, I tell myself, will be a fascinating mystery to unravel.

With two hours to kill before lunch I decide to explore further. Inactivity irritates me. There's nothing worse than sitting doing nothing. Now that I'm certain Venus knows where the missing film is hidden there's no point in me making a play of searching for it. Better to hear its whereabouts from her own lips. In fact, it will be satisfying to maneuver that revelation out of Venus' very attractive mouth. So I head out into a sunlit morning to follow the boundaries of what, after all, is my property. There's a freshness in the air I like, a crispness that makes me think of chilled champagne. Bunny doesn't rule the garden with a firm hand. The lawns are ankle deep in places, more like meadow. The green open spaces are speckled with golden dandelions. There's not much in the way of formal flowerbeds. The planting is fairly haphazard—a clump of roses there, a raft of red tulips here. A mass of violet lavender runs alongside a stretch of lush mint and lemon balm that's been allowed to grow wild and straggling, like the tresses of a fairytale hag.

As I walk down through the garden toward the boundary fence, rabbits lope off into the bushes in front of me. Not in a frightened way, but quite relaxed as if in these parts it's only a formality for the wildlife to avoid humans. Again, the sense of isolation is a strong one. There are no neighboring houses. The only road is deserted. There aren't even any jet trails in the sky. Not that I mind; this kind of retreat from civilization comes at a premium. It adds cash value to this real estate.

Marked by a post and rail fence, the boundary guides me downhill into a hollow. The forest I'd driven through yesterday extends a wooded finger into the garden itself by about a hundred paces or so. Soon I enter a shady stand of oak. There's not so much a path but a series of interconnected clearings that forms a route through the copse.

Presently the ground folds up at either side so what passes as a pathway descends into a gully. As I follow it, the sides are transformed from earth banking topped with trees to boulders that form an artificial grotto. It's probably some folly of Dad's from when he first built the house. Brambles and stinging nettles grow between the boulders. There are broken statues and stumps of pillars. No doubt it's intentional to create the appearance of an ancient Roman ruin. Here the light is greenish due to its being filtered through the leaves. The grotto forms a gloomy underworld. Vines, ivy, brambles, moss—plenty of moss; it combines to form a jade skin on the boulders. Even though I'm outdoors this is an enclosed world. The steep boulder sides are perhaps twenty feet high. Above me, at ground level, huge oaks form an ever shifting canopy of branches that, every now and again, admit a pencil-thin ray of sunlight.

Just as the sense of peace here becomes so intense I can almost reach out and touch it, a sharp snap of a sound splits the stillness. Five feet from me chips of stone burst from the boulder.

"Hey! Watch out!" I've enough wits to realize that someone's just let fly with a firearm, and the bullet's knocked a chunk out of a boulder not far from my head. "If you're hunting rabbits they're the ones with the long ears." I tug one of my own ears. "Don't you recognize a man when you see one?"

I don't see the hunter but the next shot follows within seconds of the first. This time I hear the pop of the bullet as it rips through the air near the ear I've just pulled. The bullet ricochets away down the canyon of boulders with a whine.

"*Hey!*" My yell echoes back at me.

The next shot is even closer. The rush of its slipstream tugs my hair. Whoever it is they're not hunting rabbits. I know that now. So I run forward through the grotto. A couple of shots follow in quick succession. As I run I glance up. About twenty feet above me a shadowy figure moves along the top of the canyon. They have to weave around trees and bushes along its edge so it spoils their aim. But there's no doubt who their target is.

I keep moving at a sprint. All the time I'm scanning the rock sides looking for a place to shelter. I feel like a rat scurrying inside an old bathtub. There's nowhere to hide and I'm limited to where I can run.

Although I don't take the time to idly gaze up at my pursuer I have

SHE LOVES MONSTERS

an impression of a hooded figure, either masked or with a scarf over their face. They appear to carry an automatic rifle. The chunky magazine protruding beneath it suggests that they're not going to run out of ammunition in a hurry. Beyond that I'm not dallying to check on detail. Another shot explodes the earth in front of me. I race forward. There's got to be shelter ahead, I tell myself. A fake cave, or rocky overhang. I don't plan on taking a slug in the guts, and laying down here in the dirt to watch the life ooze out of me.

"Bastard!" I yell. My God, I want to get my hands around their neck. I push myself faster. If they have to match my speed over that rough terrain up there then that's going to spoil their aim. Good. I don't want to make it easy for that piece of human filth.

A couple more shots peck chunks out of Dad's folly. They must be out of breath because the bullets fly wide of me by ten paces at least. "Useless piece of crap!" I pant. All here, take note. Berate your assailant rather than be a victim, fleeing in silence.

Then it goes wrong for me. The gully closes off into a dead end. There's a mock temple there with stone columns and a crumbling roof. It might afford protection if I could only reach it but it's built about ten feet up into the cliff face.

Only there's a miracle...a great, flaming, God-given, Christ-sponsored, archangel-underwritten miracle. Leaning against a boulder is a pump-action shotgun. My attacker's running along the top of the cliff. He's having to watch out for tangles of tree roots, so he's glancing down at his feet to avoid tripping.

Now's my wonderfully juicy opportunity. I grab the shotgun. I slide the loading mechanism. A round enters the chamber with a satisfying *snick*. Steadying my breath, I raise the shotgun and aim at the guy as he stops directly above my head. He points the rifle muzzle down at me. It's pleasing to see him jerk back a little in shock. He's seen I'm armed now. A warming glow of pleasure spreads through my stomach. Nice to provoke that reaction. Of course he's going to fire the moment I pull my trigger, only...only he has trouble with the gun. A jammed round? The mechanism isn't cocked? He takes the gun away from his shoulder so he can see what the problem is.

I settle the stock against my shoulder. Aim. Directly at the head. I squeeze the trigger. Because I'm surrounded by rock on three sides the

shotgun blast sounds like an artillery piece discharging a five-pound shell. Venting cordite gases rip leaves from the vines that cling to the rock.

What it doesn't affect is my attacker. I chamber another round and fire it at the masked figure. It doesn't even flinch. The aim is true. Only the shot doesn't hurt him. I fire again. No burst of blood and stinking guts, no scream of pain. The guy stares down at me through the slit between scarf and hood.

"Bastard!" I yell. I chamber another round then fire it directly into the cliff face. The moss ripples. I see a tiny piece of paper stick to the blast area. But no harm done. "You bastard!" I yell again. "You're a real joker, aren't you?" I shake the shotgun over my head. "You left this for me to find, didn't you? And you left it loaded with blanks! Why'd you bother with blank cartridges? Why not just leave it empty? What went wrong with your life? Did you get bored pulling wings off flies!"

Now the body language of my attacker shines with confidence. He's tricked me. He must be laughing inside until his ribs crack. Slowly now, he's in no hurry, the guy cocks the rifle, and then raises it until the muzzle points down at me. With a roar of anger I hurl the shotgun aside. "Okay. You win!" I nod with a perverse satisfaction. "Don't you get into a sweat about getting a clean shot. I'll make it easy for you." I rip open my shirt to expose my chest. "Hey, stupid. You'll find my heart just here. At the end of my finger." I touch my chest with my middle finger then flip it upright at him. If this is my last minute on Earth I'm going to use that sixty seconds to tell my assassin to go shove it.

There's a pause. Silence oozes into the grove. Though the hood is drawn over the head, so it conceals the face in shadow, I sense the guy staring at me.

I find a smile tugging at my mouth. "Hey, stupid. If you've forgotten where the trigger is, it's that iddy-biddy bit of metal sticking out of the bottom."

My murderer's deciding what to do. If there's such a thing as a moment of significance I figure it passes us by. Because a second later he raises the rifle, so the muzzle is pointing skyward, then he steps backward from the lip of the cliff and vanishes.

"Yeah," I shout. "Tell all your friends that you hunted a man for sport. A better man than you! Have a laugh about it. Because next time...do you hear me? *Next time I'll rip your head off!*"

Ten

So, this is the meal. The one that Bunny told me I'd enjoy so much. Now, despite whatever I might want to do, I find it difficult to take my eyes off Venus Lake as she ladles bright green soup into two earthenware bowls. Think of the crockery as Third World Chic and you have it. Venus is dressed in a flowing skirt of white cotton. Very nearly see-through. A little voice yattering away at the back of my head wishes it were completely transparent. Fortuitously, she's wearing a purple bodice of a flimsy material that's sheer enough to allow me teasing glimpses of her breasts. So what happened to the shy sister that's very much her brother's keeper? This version of Venus today is teasing me with glimpses of her body beneath that Gypsy-cum-hippy confection.

We're dining in the kitchen. It's ramshackle and old fashioned, but clean and homely. There's a dresser displaying bright blue plates. The kitchen is cavernous and full of roast meat smells from the huge iron oven. There's a trace of spice hanging on the air. I've already taken my place at the farmhouse table and I'm hungrily anticipating the feast.

There's a terrific topic of conversation I can open with. *Someone tried to murder me this morning. And just for a joke they left me a gun loaded with blanks. Isn't that the most deliciously witty jape you've ever heard of?* But, no. I don't mention it. I'll save that revelation for later. Because I'm watching the way she walks. My intentions are purely wolfish. To confess a gunman tried to blow holes in my heart will be an ideal tool to win her sympathy this evening when the time is right. Did I say wolfish? Yes, I lust manfully after her. No doubting that.

SHE LOVES MONSTERS

She's beautiful. Believe me, I don't want to be cruel to her. I want her to like me.

"How are your fingers?" she asks.

"Fine." I glance at the reddened skin with the singed hairs. She's looking, too, with concern on that pretty, elfin face. I add, "You're confident your brother won't try to burn us all alive in our beds again tonight?"

"I've locked him in his room."

"Oh."

"Bread?"

"Just a slice."

She cuts a piece from a gargantuan dome of golden brown loaf.

I add, "And confiscated all his matches and firearms?"

As she sits she glances sharply at me. "He doesn't own any guns."

"Glad to hear it. Interesting looking soup." I nod at the bowl of brilliant green liquid.

"It's made from nettles."

"The same ones Mr. Happy Bunny and I cut this morning?"

"Why waste them? Nettles are good for you. One of the most mineral-rich vegetables you can eat."

I peer into the bilious green and see my reflection gazing back. "Then you can have them carve *She Fed Him Poison Weeds* on my gravestone."

"Cooking destroys the poison."

"An old country recipe, I suppose."

"I found it on the internet. Gently fry the nettle tops in oil, add vegetable stock and seasoning, and then liquefy in the blender."

I eat a spoonful. "Not bad. Tastes a bit like spinach." I glance up as she breaks her slice of bread in two. There's a kind of energy in the woman that was absent yesterday when she was as timid as the proverbial mouse. It's as if she's found the dial to her internal rheostat and cranked up the voltage. So why the change?

I lean sideways a little so I can see one of her bare feet against the stone floor. Her toes are puffy. The skin is mottled with pinks and whites.

"Venus. You stung your feet badly down at the barn this morning. What made you walk through the nettles?"

"Last year I broke my ankle. The poison in stinging nettles is a remedy for conditions like rheumatism and arthritis. Its anti-inflammatory properties have been used for thousands of years. You can also treat snakebites and asthma with preparations made from them."

"So you deliberately sting yourself? Masochistic, don't you think?"

"From time-to-time my ankle still aches and I find nettle stings stop it from hurting."

I have to smile at this. "If it works for you." There's a pause as we eat then I ask, "How many nettles would you need to treat a broken neck?"

"I'm sorry, Mr. Calner, I don't understand."

"Don't go back to Mr. Calner. Call me Jack."

"Jack." She nods, accepting the invitation to use my first name.

I press on. "I was curious if nettles would cure major injuries because yesterday you nearly wound up with a broken neck when you ran into my car. Why did you do that?"

"I run because the exercise is good for me."

"You mean you always go jogging in the nude?"

"It's attaining parity with nature. To me, that's important."

Expansion on a theme. Elaboration of the facts. If I'd been expecting Venus, pretty fawn-eyed Venus Lake, to get all evangelical about the merits of dashing through the woods in her birthday suit I'm mistaken. Instead she fires back a question at me. Her tone is pleasant, she's smiling, but I sense currents of fire in her veins now.

"Jack. What are your plans for my brother's film?"

I feign ignorance. "If I find it."

"If you find it," she nods while holding my gaze.

"Christopher Lake fans have been waiting for years to see it. It ranks alongside Lon Chaney's *London After Midnight* as one of the legendary lost films. So…" I set down my spoon beside the bowl. "It will be worth millions. I plan a theatrical release. Cinemas worldwide. There'll be a collector's edition DVD to follow, then a regular release. A coffee table tie-in book. I'll exploit the photo library stills from the film for use in commercials, clothing and whatever merchandise I deem appropriate."

"And 'appropriate' means anything that will turn a profit?"

"Absolutely."

SHE LOVES MONSTERS

"My brother sacrificed his health for that film."

"With the intention of earning money from it. Even Da Vinci and Van Gogh painted with the intention of reaping cash from their art. Christopher is no exception." I smile. "Think of *Vorada* becoming an epidemic like the flu. It's going to infect the cinema-going public. It'll saturate the TV-watching and DVD-collecting world. Everyone will see your brother's masterpiece. And when the theatre prints are worn out I'm going to slice them, mount them and sell them frame by frame to the fans. This is really satisfying soup, by the way."

"You have Bunny to thank for it."

"Happy, smiling Bunny. Why is he brimming with sheer bloody joy all the time?"

"Because forty years ago he saved the world."

"Bunny's a superhero? My-oh-my." This brings a smile to my own face. "Go on, Venus, break it to me. How?" I bite off a chunk of bread.

"He killed his family." She says this matter-of-factly before spooning that audaciously green soup into her mouth.

I suspect a leg pull. "Bunny bumped-off his family? So you're harboring a murderer?"

As if recounting a banal event, she shrugs. "When he was nineteen he killed his parents in their sleep, then he set fire to the house."

"In the lunacy stakes that is spectacular."

"No. There weren't any symptoms of mental illness. None of the malaise or distorted perceptions associated with schizophrenia, or any other indicators of psychosis. Neither were drugs or alcohol involved."

"Why'd he do it then? For the inheritance?"

"Bunny told me that on his nineteenth birthday he became convinced that his parents were infected with a virus that would decimate the human race."

"So he barbecued Ma and Pa."

She nods.

I continue spooning the soup into my mouth. "Like I said. Nuts. Has to be."

"Psychiatrists couldn't diagnose a mental condition. They said he was sane so the judge sent him to prison. Bunny was a model prisoner; they released him on license ten years ago."

"Let's get this straight." I'm still amused by the notion of the mass-murderer harvesting nettles for my soup. Talk about adding a certain *je ne sais quoi*. "Bunny convinced himself his mother and father were plague carriers. That to save the human race he must destroy them and the bug, so he slaughtered them and burnt their bodies. Then he spent the next thirty years of his life behind bars?"

"Yes."

"Then why the devil is he so infernally happy all the time?"

"Don't you see? In his heart of hearts, Bunny believes he saved the human race by destroying a lethal virus."

"But there was no bloody virus."

"Bunny believes that there was. He knew he couldn't convince the authorities that was the case, so he sacrificed his liberty for the good of humankind."

"And to this day Bunny thinks he saved our skins by incinerating his parents?"

"Yes. That's why he's happy. He had the courage to risk everything in his life to spare the world from plague. In his eyes he succeeded."

"Wow." I say this in an understated way to show her I'm not living in awe of Bunny's accomplishments.

"Jack, I know I can't make you understand how Bunny feels," she tells me. "But Bunny has this supreme…*absolute* self-confidence. Bunny knows he has the power to save the world. How many of us can claim we're able to do that?"

I finish the last spoonful of soup. "That's not power, that's self-delusion. Delicious bread by the way. I'll bet it's home baked. Did Bunny's superhero fingers knead the dough? "

"I've roasted lamb for the main course."

"I had you down for a vegetarian."

"Then it proves you know nothing about me, Jack."

She stands and collects the bowls from the table. When she reaches out for my spoon beside the bowl I close my hand over hers. "Venus. You and your brother will make a lot of money out of the film. You know that?"

At that moment I want to grip her so hard in my arms that it makes her gasp. I picture myself kissing her lips. That sheer naked WANTING. It's so powerful that my heart hammers. The same moment I imagine myself kissing her I also see her rejecting me. It's an

SHE LOVES MONSTERS

agony-ecstasy moment. What if she is physically repelled by me? The idea is so unnerving. So unusual. I've not experienced anything like it before, but at that instant I shudder with fear. I am terrified of being rejected by her. Even the film I've fought to take possession of seems unimportant. For me, it's heresy to turn my back on the opportunity to make money. But: I WANT VENUS LAKE. The truth is as simple and as stark as that.

It can only have been seconds, yet it seems I've been resting my hand on hers for whole minutes. With those fawn-like brown eyes she looks into mine. I can't read what she's thinking from her expression. Her face is a mask—okay, a beautiful mask—but she's not allowing any emotion to escape the armor plating.

In that painful, suspended moment, where time slips away through the window to be replaced by this painful longing in my chest, I hear a rising surge of applause and voices calling. I glance toward the doorway. The eerie notes of an accordion wind through the corridor and into the kitchen. On the heels of that comes a male voice singing in French. The song rises in volume until it takes possession of the room.

Venus slips her hand from beneath mine, then moves away to put the bowls and cutlery in the sink. As the resonant voice surges through the house, singing a song that appears to quiver with profundity, Venus tosses words back to me over her shoulder. "That's Christopher's favorite song...*Amsterdam*...the singer's Jacques Brel. There's potatoes and spring cabbage...is that okay?"

"I'm fine with anything. As long as there's no garlic. I hate garlic."

Things are changing. Venus telling me Bunny is a parent killer, who thinks he's saved the world. My feelings...*no*...my *desires* for Venus. My fear of her rejecting me. The song that's...well...so haunting...so incredibly haunting. Not only is all that transforming the environment I find myself in, but I also feel a difference inside myself. Fear? Lack of confidence? No, I never experience those states of mind. But in the last few minutes I sense I'm different inside. It's hard to put my finger on it. I'm more tentative. Instead of firing off the string of authoritative statements that is my norm, I'm considering what to say before I open my mouth. For a moment back there I'd planned to stand up and kiss Venus. A full, passionate, searing kiss that would have signaled to her what my intentions were.

Now?

Well, now I sit at the table in this rustic kitchen with the song gusting through the fabric of my father's house like a cavalcade of ghosts.

I say nothing. Venus moves to the oven to lift out a sizzling leg of lamb. The smell of roasting meat has an intensity I don't remember experiencing before. And the song starts again. The same song. Jacques Brel's *Amsterdam*. My heart's beating hard. The music is insinuating itself into my mind. I can't take my eyes off Venus. Her calves are so slender beneath that skirt. She hurled her naked body into the path of my car.

Wait a minute. What did I say just then? What was it? Because it wasn't true. I described this as my father's house. No. Correction. My father is dead. Montage is my house.

Venus sets the steaming leg of lamb on the table. The brown meat bubbles with aromatic juices. After that she puts a large knife in front of me. "You can carve while I finish the vegetables."

So as Venus moves back and forth from stove to sink, draining vegetables and adding butter to potatoes, I carve thick, glistening slices of lamb. Meanwhile, the Jacques Brel song still ghosts through the house. A hymn to sailors, to dancing, bloodshed and to the whores in the port of Amsterdam. All this and a glimpse of the eternal, too. Or so Venus tells me as she drains the cabbage.

You're going to have to do something about finding the film—and do something about Venus. This is what I tell myself as I cut the meat. And I know I've got to do it soon. Because I suspect that Venus Lake has developed plans all of her own.

Eleven

I'm sitting in my room. The one beneath the bronze dome. The sun is incredibly bright as it piles in through the windows. When I shield my eyes I can look over the lawns to the meadows, forests and the hills in the distance. I didn't have alcohol with the lunch Venus prepared. The meal was satisfying, perhaps so satisfying I feel sluggish, yet my fingers and face are tingling. I find myself repeating the same banal thought for no particular reason. "*Vorada* will require a cinematograph." And again: "*Vorada* will need a cinematograph."

But what is a cinematograph? Some mechanical device employed by a cinema, I suppose. But it's that word: CINEMATOGRAPH. An odd word full of lumpy syllables. I imagine Orson Welles' deep, rumbling voice enunciating the word through clouds of cigar smoke. "Mr. Jack Calner," Orson says to me, "Jack, if I may call you Jack? Let me tell you, Jack. When you find that lost film it will be necessary to employ a cinematograph."

I chuckle. "Cinematograph." My face tingles and I rub it vigorously. "Nettles. Nettle soup." My head shakes. "The nettles are stinging me from the inside." My head is so heavy…it's weighed down by the word CINEMATOGRAPH. All those syllables like so many lumps of iron.

The weight of it all draws my face downward so I'm staring at the pattern in the rug. Suddenly, it seems a long way off. It's all random swirls and blocks of color. I see a face in a clump of tangerine colored blotches. It's an earnest face. The face of a young man. The expression radiates the emotion that the owner of the face has some vital message to impart to me.

SHE LOVES MONSTERS

I lick my lips. They're tingling, too. A rumbustious tingling. Prick, prick, prick. The face in the rug locks its eyes on me. The lips move but I can't hear any sound.

"Hello," I say, as if faces appearing from rugs happens to me every day and twice on Sundays. "What have you got to tell me?"

"Get out!" The face dissolves into a stream of tangerine light rays.

"Hmmm." I lick my lips. "Hmm. Nettle soup." My eyes tingle. "I think I'm allergic." My hands are so numb that I rub my fingers together as if trying to remove a sticky juice from the tips. "I don't feel…hmm." Now I'm distracted by my hands. The backs of them are too big. The pores have become a series of pits in the skin. Hairs bristle with the thickness and blackness of sea urchin spines. *"Rest."* With an odd abruptness I throw myself back from my sitting position on the bed to lying flat on the mattress.

The sunlight grows more intense. It's as if the room cascades with molten gold. Its brilliance goes beyond magnitude. The light has been transfigured. The tingling I experience in the irises of my eyes dances along the optic nerve to scintillate and coruscate amid the roomy, billowing, delicious folds of my brain. When I close my eyes the light isn't diminished. It grows brighter…brighter…

Funny this… Not funny ha-ha… Previously, I believed I had an excellent vocabulary. But now I know those words were like buds on a plant. As I lie here I realize the tightly budded words are blossoming into their full meaning. My native tongue was a foreign language to me.

Twelve

The instant I wake I look at the clock on the bedside table. Six o'clock on the nail. The evening sun floods the room. With insight blazing through my head I know the truth. That meal I ate. Venus Lake spiked it. There have been times I've drunk so much whisky that it's all but wiped clean my mind. What I experienced before I fell asleep this afternoon was nothing like being drunk. There was no diminishment of intelligence. No slurring or staggering. Instead, perceptions altered. My hands had appeared the size of table tops. The rug on the floor had seemed a hundred yards away before the human face had appeared to grow out of it. That, my friend, was hallucination for sure. I was seeing things that simply did not exist in the real world. So what else do I know as I sit here, staring at the clock? Venus slipped a drug into my meal with a specific purpose in mind. All part of her master plan. But what plan is that? Venus possesses the lost film. She pretends she doesn't. Her insane brother knows she has it, too. He urged me to find it before "she can use it." Venus, however, has drugged me so she can move *Vorada* to a new hiding place.

Whereas I should be punching the pillow while cursing Venus Lake for dropping LSD into my soup I also know another fact—that great big glittering not-to-be-denied fact. And that fact is: I long to get hold of her. No, not to do her violence. But to hold her. To say sweet and gentle things to her. The truth is I've never responded like this to a woman before. This state of mind should trouble me. The thing is when I picture her I'm filled with a warming goodness that is so alien to me.

I clench my fists. What now? I can't just drive away with a forgiving smile splashed all across my face. There are questions to be answered. I've got to confront her and hear from her lips why she drugged me—and learn her intentions for the film. "Ask her what the hell is a cinematograph, too." The line I speak aloud makes me pause. I study my hands—both backs and palms. The lines in the skin are deep as creeks. Fingernails are as broad and as glossy as polished window glass. My lips tingle.

I breathe deeply. "Take it easy, Jack. You're not clear of it yet."

For a moment I'm compelled to examine my hands. They have an allure that's both monstrous and beautiful. They repel me but I'm driven to keep staring at these blood-filled extremities as I rotate them, so I can see them back and palm. I bite my lip. "You've got to give it to her, Jack. She's spiked you good." The tingle spreads along my arms. "Hmm. Cinematograph." I give a savage shake of my head. "Don't start that again, Jack. Don't you dare."

I stand upright and move to the window as if I'm carried through the air. There's no sensation of walking. I've not used drugs before. This must be one of the effects. There may be more. I must be on my guard. A second later I'm at the window. As deeply as I can I inhale. Fresh air might dispel the narcotic from my veins. At the second lungful of air I see a figure run across the sunlit lawn. With the sun shining in my eyes I have to shield them with my hand.

It's her. Venus Lake. Running once more. Slim legs a blur. Brown hair fluttering. Naked body shining.

"She's at it again." I murmur. That nude cross country run fetish of hers that brought her in bruising collision with my car.

Then the insane idea. No, not idea. This mad compulsion. Run after Venus Lake. Stop her. Grab her by the shoulders. Don't let go until she tells you why she drugged you. Get her to confess where she's hidden the film. FORCE HER!

That lightness in my body makes running effortless. I fly for the bedroom door that contracts from Gulliver huge to Alice Through The Looking Glass miniscule. Shouldn't have poisoned you with that muck, Jack. She's no right to trick you into eating acid…trippy, dippy, hippy acid…

The door swells into normality as I reach it. A moment later I'm through it. I don't stagger. I'm not clumsy. My mind isn't cloudy. This sensation isn't like knocking back a pot full of booze. My thoughts are sharp as a razor. Only they're stretched into different shapes. Perspectives are skewed. The light possesses different qualities. Dimensions have been rearranged. As I speed toward the stairs, I hear applause.

For me.

Cheers.

They're my adulation.

Then I know what it is. Venus's mad hatter brother is playing his music again. It's the same wheezing call of the accordion. Jacques Brel sings the opening verse of *Amsterdam*. The volume swells as I zoom downstairs without seemingly making contact with the risers. Then as the voice grows in passion, and those French words about love and death and obsession blow through my head, I hurtle through the hallway, through the living room with its mosaic and marble statues of gods and monsters and heroes. And then I'm through the door onto the patio. There's the burn mark where I kicked out the blazing chair last night. Way off to my right I glimpse the silver head of Bunny—smiling, mass-murdering Bunny the gardener. He's wiping the blade of the scythe. Then he returns to slaughtering a whole family of nettles. Just for a second he pauses as he watches me run across the lawn in pursuit of his mistress. After that, he returns to his rhythmic work. As measured as a metronome. Sweep, cut, swish. The curving blade fells a dozen nettles in a stroke. The green blood of the plants drips from sharp steel.

Jacques Brel's song fades slowly as I race away from Montage. I glance back to see Christopher Lake standing in the window of his room. The man's empty stare follows me across the lawn. Then I look forward again as I zigzag past bushes in my hunt for that strange guy's naked sister. The sun is much lower. Its brilliance dazzles. She was here. This is where I saw her from the window. My pace slows to a near standstill. Her perfume haunts the spaces between the trees. In my mind the scent takes the shape of her beautiful figure. I step into it to envelop myself in that sweetened atmosphere.

A desperation takes hold of me. I'll never see her again. She's gone. That sense of loss is almost overwhelming. Just as I believe I'll crumble to the earth there and then I catch a glimpse of her behind a line of poplars. Once more an unnatural energy fires me up. I'm running before I've even thought about doing so. My feet don't seem to touch the ground. This is an effortless glide just above the grass. Ahead of me I catch glimpses of her silhouette. The sun is dazzlingly low in the sky. All I make out is the flick of her long hair. That and the pale flash of the bare soles of her feet.

I call out, "Venus!" She doesn't seem to hear. "Venus, stop! I need to talk to you."

Stop. Talk. Conversation. A civilized exchange of statements. But it doesn't feel like that now. This is a chase. I'm the hunter! It's The Powerful versus The Powerless. A formidable strength fills my body. That energy drives my legs. In my arms is the power to uproot trees and topple mountains.

It's the drug. You knew it could have more effects. You're running. The narcotic is moving faster through your bloodstream. Beware, beware, beware... *Don't do anything that will cause harm.* These words resonate. Because that's the feeling...that's the TASTE in my mouth. I have become dangerous.

DANGEROUS.

In my drug altered state...my mind is reconfigured. The word DANGEROUS has a dozen new definitions. Didn't I tell you that until now words had been tightly budded things with a constricted meaning? Now the words are opening. Blossoming. Their meaning is expanding all the time. Take DANGEROUS for instance. It's become a magic word. I am dangerous. That means I can perform acts that no other man can. Danger is the key to giving me what I want. Danger is power. The power of danger has the ability to destroy old boundaries, it can smash moribund ideas and annihilate redundant systems. With this dangerous, destructive power I can obliterate the old and build anew.

Hunt her. Catch her. Hold Venus by those lovely naked shoulders. Tell her exactly what will happen to her.

THEN DO IT!

Thirteen

We're running along the boundary of the property. I catch teasing glimpses of her bare skin. But most of the time she's concealed by bushes…another time she's running through open ground. Only the grass is so tall it comes to her shoulder blades. The bruise on her shoulder is plain to see. The one dealt to her by smacking into the front of my car.

Venus. Venus. Venus. In my mind her name is fire. Its heat drives through my flesh.

And I'm gaining on her. We've run around the perimeter of the grounds. Her arms, legs, head and back are a blur. The bare skin is a shining miracle. I have to touch it soon. Very, very soon. Not just touch either. Grip. Clutch in my strong fingers.

Rabbits hop aside as she runs through a group of them. Birds fly from branches near her until sometimes it seems she's haloed by the flapping wings of white doves. Then she's moving through the trees again, along the path that takes her into the finger of woodland that penetrates the garden. I've been here before. I know it. I know where it leads. That gully. The steep-sided valley of boulders with no exit. The sheltering oaks.

What I describe next is contradictory, but it's nothing less than a metaphor for my experiences here at Montage. Even though I can fully see her body I don't see her in entirety. The dappling shadows, the spots of sunlight, they simultaneously illuminate her and hide her. It's a light that has the power to transform her once again. The first time I'd seen Venus after the car had struck her and she'd raced away into the forest

SHE LOVES MONSTERS

I'd fancied she'd become part panther. Again she becomes almost feline; a beautiful, supple figure that moves with undulating grace through a confusion of light and shade. She glides deeper into the forest.

I know this place only too well. I've been here before. This is where the gunman tried to kill me. Then the terrifying thought: What if he's lying in wait again with his rifle? This vividly sculptured piece of woman flesh. Gorgeous, lithe, with the fawn-like eyes beneath a wash of brown hair. What value would he award to a target such as that? What will he do when he sees a beautiful woman racing toward him without so much as a scrap of cloth to cover her nakedness? I imagine him drawing back the rifle bolt with a gloating smile.

"Venus!" Her name is thunder on my lips. "Venus! Don't go down there. It's dangerous!"

Dangerous. But aren't I the danger? Aren't I a thundering, raging bull of a man who is the sole threat to this vulnerable human being?

"Venus." I pause to bellow, "STOP!"

But I've paused too long. She's escaping me. Within seconds she's vanished into the deep-sided gully.

In no time at all, I run into the man-made valley; the sound of my feet pound back at me from the rock sides. I've been a mere moment. I've been so quick. So why is it she's vanished from the face of the earth?

That drug…that mutilator of reality…is still polluting my bloodstream. Down here in the gully my perception of the world is mangled out of shape. The stone slabs that form the path appear to undulate like the scaled back of a long, sinuous boa constrictor. Boulders swell to the size of trucks. The valley sides could be a mile high at either side of me. Above them, tree trunks soar up into leafy branches that now form a ceiling that's nothing less than an incandescent green. I can smell the moss so strongly it becomes an electric current running up my nostrils into my head to tingle the nerves in my brain. And amid this psychedelic hub-hub of shifting colors and coalescing shades of green, where is Venus Lake? The naked beauty who poisons men's food. Narcotic inveigler.

I look at my hands again. The fingers are as long and thin as bamboo canes. Yet the joints are bulbous mouth shapes with shouting lips. The veins beneath the skin are purple highways. I fancy I see blood platelets scurrying through them, each one being piggy-backed by molecules of the narcotic. Little parasites. Dirty little parasites. As I rub the palms of my hands against my hips I feel an object in my pocket. My cell phone. Quickly, I drag it out and switch it on. Uncanny. The cane-like fingers still possess their old dexterity. On screen the directory throws up my business partner's name. I thumb the call button. And I'm standing there in the wash of jade light. At both sides of me rise the rocky cliffs to the emerald heaven above.

"Where have you disappeared, Venus? Where have you gone..." I'm singing the words under my breath. "Watch out, watch out, there's a man-shooter about." This is funny. I press a hand to my lips to block laughter bubbling from my mouth. A ring tone is merrily tootling away, then a voice in my ear.

"Jack. I've been trying to phone you for the last ten hours. Where the hell are you?"

"Steiger—"

"Do you have the film? Because I've got some guys from Hollywood chomping at the bit. They'll pay a ten million finder's fee over and above the rights sale. Did you hear that, Jack?"

"Steiger... Steiger. Listen. She's poisoned me. Isn't that just so brilliant!"

"You're talking about Venus Lake?"

"She put some stuff in the soup... Lord, it was the greenest soup I've ever seen in my life."

"She's poisoned you? Hell, Jack. Don't do anything. I'll get the police and an ambulance. Don't do anything. Just wait there!"

"Steiger. Isn't that wonderful? The woman spiked my food."

"Wait until you get medical help."

"And then this morning a guy tried to pick me off with a rifle. I'm standing here in the forest and I'm looking at where the bullet went—SMACK!—into a rock. Look, I can put my finger in the hole. That would have blown my head all over the place."

"You're still at Montage. Right?"

"Absolutely."

"I'll get help to you there."

"No."

SHE LOVES MONSTERS

"What?"

"No, don't you dare, Steiger. No police."

"Jack, you said you'd been poisoned. If this is a joke it's not funny."

"Venus Lake shoved acid...LSD? It must be LSD; she shoved it into my food. I'm high. Everything looks weird. Either too big or too small or out of shape...or things like trees seem to be lit from the inside. The light is blinding. But I can think clearly. I'm lucid."

"You don't sound lucid."

"I'm fine. My mind's a razor... I've never known it so sharp."

"But if she's tried to kill you—"

"Not kill me. She'd have done something else...arsenic, or Bunny. Maybe the burning chair. You know, toxic fumes."

"Jack, look, for God sakes, listen to me. What you're telling me isn't making any sense. Go lie down. I'll phone the police from here. Then I'll drive up to Montage with a couple of the guys."

"Don't do anything. Do nothing." I take a deep breath and rush the words out before he can speak. "I can use this, Steiger. Venus Lake could end up in jail for doing this to me. This is my lever. I'll get her to bring the film to me. And then I'll renegotiate the contract. Currently, we have to split the proceeds fifty-fifty with Christopher Lake. I'll get her to sign a rider to the contract altering the profit split seventy-thirty in our favor."

Poison. Shootings. Drug trips. That's all well and good, but just you talk money to Steiger—that's when his mind really begins to focus. "Okay, Jack. As long as you know what you're doing. If they try anything else on you call the police. Got that?"

"Don't worry, my funny little friend." The endearment tickles me. I have to clamp my hand over my mouth to stop laughing out loud. "I'm big enough to look after myself."

"Okay, but watch your back. Did you hear me? *Watch your back.*"

I switch off the phone and slip it back into my pocket.

"I forgot to tell you one thing." I murmur these words under my breath as my heart slams against my ribs. "I like Venus Lake. She's amazing..." And, don't you know it? The only ears that hear my once-in-a-lifetime confession are affixed to the heads of furry woodland animals.

I move forward again. The valley walls close in. I glimpse fragments of stone lintel and columns that convey the fantasy that this was the site of a ruined temple. Now stone arms are outstretched from the rock. Gleaming white marble with delicate fingers. They reach out to touch my face as I pass. That drug. It's trickling hallucinatory thoughts into my head again. Now I see the carved head of a woman jutting from the moss level with my own face. Her eyes are closed but all of a sudden her mouth drops open as if to call at me. A curse? A blessing? A warning? There's no human voice. It's the same sound as a seashell placed against your ear. Only louder…far louder…than you've heard before. It rises to a wail as blood begins to pour from the yawning mouth.

How long will this drug stay in my body? It's got to pass soon.

By now I've reached the end of the gully. There's no way forward. And no way up to the top of the cliffs which hem me in at both sides as sheer as prison walls. There's the mock temple again. I see the black smudge on the boulder where I fired the shotgun blank this morning. Up there had stood the rifleman. The big tease. He pretended to make a play of shooting me then scuttled away. My gaze travels up the moss-covered rock face to a million tree roots bursting like monstrous tentacles from the earth above me. And there are the tree trunks. Above them, the mobile canopy of branches that make a sizzling sound as the evening breeze stirs the leaves. And it's green…all so very green… Vertigo tugs at me. I'm lightheaded.

Then it's her. As if she's been there for the last hundred years. For decades she's remained rooted there like one of those trees. And yet all along…all down through those waiting, watchful, just-biding-her-time years…she's known I'd come walking along this gully to find her there, haloed by an emerald radiance.

She must still be naked. With the light behind her all I see is her silhouette. Her hair flutters. Those soft doe eyes glint from the shadow and I know…I KNOW…she's watching me.

"Venus." I meet the gaze head on. "You've got to come down here."

She says nothing. Golden dust motes glide with aching slowness on green rays of light.

Louder, I say, "Come down here where I can I talk to you."

"No, Jack. That won't be a good idea."

"Why?"

SHE LOVES MONSTERS

"Call it intuition, but I sense you're liable to do things now that you wouldn't dream of doing at any other time."

"Come down here. You can trust me."

"Not until the acid's worn off. It's working on the barriers inside your head, Jack. For the next couple of hours you'll be capable of anything."

The woozy sense of floating through the forest is being replaced by a burning need to have my questions answered.

"Venus. You put something in my food. What was it?"

"The 'what' is less important than the 'why.'"

"You wanted me out of the way for a few hours so you could move the film to some place where I couldn't find it. Isn't that right?"

"No."

Still she doesn't move during this surreal conversation. Me, at the bottom of a gully adorned with mock temple ruins, addressing the naked woman in tantalizing silhouette at the top of the cliff. Only the knowledge that she is…for the moment…beyond my reach exerts a corrosive effect on my nerves. For the first time since waking this afternoon an edginess unsettles me. I realize I've lost control of events here at Montage. I came here to see the house that my father left me, and to lay claim to Christopher Lake's famously lost *Vorada*. Knowing that Venus has outmaneuvered me prickles my ego, to say the least.

"So why did you decide to spice up the broth with a narcotic?"

"To remove inhibitions. When you hear what I'm going to tell you next I want you to absorb the information differently than how you usually do."

"Okay, you're going to tell me something amazing. Come down here and share it with me properly."

"Jack, right now you're capable of committing acts that you wouldn't normally dream of. That will soon pass, but until it does you'll be a danger to me."

"You can trust me. I'm still loveable Jack Calner."

"You've never EVER been loveable Jack Calner."

"So why put your dirty drug in my food, then?"

"Creative destruction."

"Did I hallucinate what you said right then? You did say 'creative destruction?'"

"Does it mean anything to you?"

"It means crap all." Suddenly the lights are greener; the cliff face is taller. The moss is fascinating beyond words. I must stare at it. I have to watch a turquoise and sea green phosphorescence spiraling through it. It's a fact. I'm not free of these chemicals yet.

"Creative destruction," she says matter-of-factly. "That's an academic phrase coined by the Austrian economist Joseph Schumpeter. Put another way, it's evidence for every cloud having a silver lining. In order for civilization to advance conventional ideas, machines, technologies, social models become obsolete; they are regularly destroyed, and are replaced by something newer and better. Look at the financial news: Over ten percent of all companies in America vanish every twelve months. It affects biology, too. More than ninety-nine percent of all species that have lived on this planet are now extinct. Creative destruction is what makes progress possible."

"This is weird." I shake my head as the vertigo returns. "You're up there lecturing to me—naked. I'm down here—not understanding."

"Jack. Society is stagnating. Progress is slowing down. It's because we as nations in the Western world have contrived to get ourselves in a rut. When there are wars...and I'm talking about major conflicts here...technology leaps forward, society goes into a state of meltdown, but then emerges a new, dynamic model with an abundance of inventions available to the masses."

"For example?"

"Before World War One nearly every household had at least one maid. After the war only the rich employed servants, not only because the very fabric of society had changed but the advent of affordable appliances meant there was no need to employ domestic staff. When World War Two started we had piston-engine biplanes that took off from cow fields. By the end of the war the old flying machines were being replaced by jet aircraft that could see through fog and darkness using radar. They landed on concrete runways. Soon they'd be breaking the sound barrier. Ten years after that, ordinary men and women could board passenger jets to fly the world over."

"You're saying that if it weren't for the World Wars we'd still be hitching our crusty old mule to a cart?"

"And now we ride around in cars. But even the latest models

employ stagnant technology now. Progress is becoming sluggish. There should be a cure for cancer, only we're losing the will to find it."

"You know, Venus. You weren't at all like this yesterday when I first met you. And I'm not just speaking of your lack of clothes." I catch a glimpse of a gleaming, naked hip. "You played dumb, didn't you? So I'd underestimate you?"

"It's not only wars. When individuals who the public adore are killed they become martyrs. That in turn empowers people. They achieve the impossible to honor their martyred hero."

"Like?"

"President Kennedy. Do you think his promise to land a man on the moon in less than a decade would have been fulfilled if he'd lived? He'd have become just another retired politician playing golf all day. When Kennedy made the promise he was only trying to raise the public's spirits. Even he didn't believe a moon landing would happen."

"But he died—and it did."

"Yes."

"Hmm. Now let me get this straight. You tricked me into eating a potful of drugs so you could give me this lecture. Me down here. Baffled. You up there—naked as the day you were born. I'll tell you this, Venus, I'm feeling pretty wacky on this stuff at the moment. You know…hell…talking statues, gooseberry skies, marshmallow stones." I squeeze a boulder with my fingers. For me it's rubbery rather than rigid. "I know I'm hallucinating…but come on, you can tell Jack your master plan."

"The drug reduces the patterns of resistance you've built up inside your head since childhood. Everyone develops these systems of 'disbelief' to protect them from radical new ideas. If I'd explained all this about creative destruction without the chemical in your bloodstream you would have processed this information in your habitual way. Which would have been negative and disbelieving, to say the least."

"Who says I believe you now?"

"You won't immediately, but the facts will sidestep the mental barriers that resist radical, and therefore troubling, ideas."

"Excuse me, Venus, for pointing this out. But I don't recollect you telling me any earthshaking ideas."

"No, this is it. This film of Christopher's…"

"*Vorada*...originally called *I Am Your Death*. Cheerful title. Cheerful as body bags." The greens of moss and leaves are turning very green again.

"*Vorada* has certain qualities."

"Go on."

"Some people watching it will come to understand the necessity for creative destruction. They'll realize that it will be ultimately beneficial for humankind if they start a war. Or kill a prominent public figure. A death that will create a martyr. Just as Lee Harvey Oswald made a martyr of Kennedy."

"Venus. My lovely, lovely Venus. You've lived in isolation for too long. That can play tricks on people, you know?"

"If you promise to help me, I'll give you *Vorada*."

"It's mine anyway."

Her voice softens. "You can have whatever else you want, too."

As I look up at the silhouette against the emerald splash of leaves she steps forward into the light. Then she moves back into the shadows again.

But I've seen her. I've set my eyes on every inch of her shining nakedness. The beauty of her body winds me. I stand there breathless for a full minute. Thoughts whirl inside my head. Possibilities. So much is within reach now. I only need the courage to reach out and take it. A thought occurs to me: If I run back along the gully now, can I catch her before she makes it back to the house?

So, this is it. I race along that crease in the woodland floor. My drug enhanced senses revel in the greenery of its vines, grass, plants, lichens, moss—so much velvety, jade moss—the trees and marble debris of mock temples. All that and the marbled whiteness of statues of Greek gods and goddesses. Colors, scents, sounds are so much more vibrant. When this drug leaves my system will the world seem a poor, gray thing in comparison? Now the sound of birdsong swells—the excited piping, shrills, whistles, hoots and love calls. It fills the forest. Just as I think the sound will overwhelm me it suddenly collapses into silence.

Standing there in front of me, blocking my way, his eyes locked on mine, is a figure with a gun.

I stop dead twenty paces from the man. "So...you've come to finish what you started?" I see Christopher Lake standing there. He's wearing a brown leather jacket over a naked torso. His lower half is clad in faded denim jeans. He's barefoot.

"What is it with you Lakes and clothes? Or rather the lack of them?"

The automatic rifle he holds is the same model I saw this morning. A chunky magazine extends downward from beneath it, no doubt packed full of nice, shining high-velocity ammo.

"What are you waiting for, Christopher? Still haven't got the guts to shoot me in the head?" I extend my arms in a crucifixion pose. "Why not start at the fingertips? Then, blasting merrily away, work in toward the center. That's where the lungs and heart are. Understand?"

I look over his shoulder in case Venus has noticed that her brother's on one of his nutty frolics. But she's vanished back to the house. I turn back to meet Christopher's eye. This cult film director—a living legend for critics and fans alike—is panting. He's unsure of himself. There's an edginess there as if he's only holding it together with a supreme effort of will. He's gripping the gun by the barrel close to its muzzle with one hand; the other's at the end of the stock. The rifle's pointing upward. It looks like it feels alien to him. I tell him, "You did a better job of handling that weapon this morning, didn't you? What went wrong? Afraid it might bite?"

Twitchy, he flicks a glance back at the house.

Then the great, shining bells and whistles of revelation burst over me. "That wasn't you this morning, was it?"

He turns to me, tremors running across his face. "What?"

"You weren't the one trying to kill me. You can't even hold a rifle properly."

With a jerky abruptness he moves the rifle. It's not pointing at me. But it's getting close. I keep an eye on his trigger finger. It's still curled around the rifle's body.

"You, Christopher, were locked in your bedroom. No. It was Venus who was playing games with the rifle this morning. Isn't that right?"

He nods. There's a scared expression on his face. His body language is edgy. He's expecting to be discovered…or even attacked.

"So what's your sister doing taking pot shots at her house guest? I'm only trying to make the pair of you rich. Because you haven't got a penny between you, have you?"

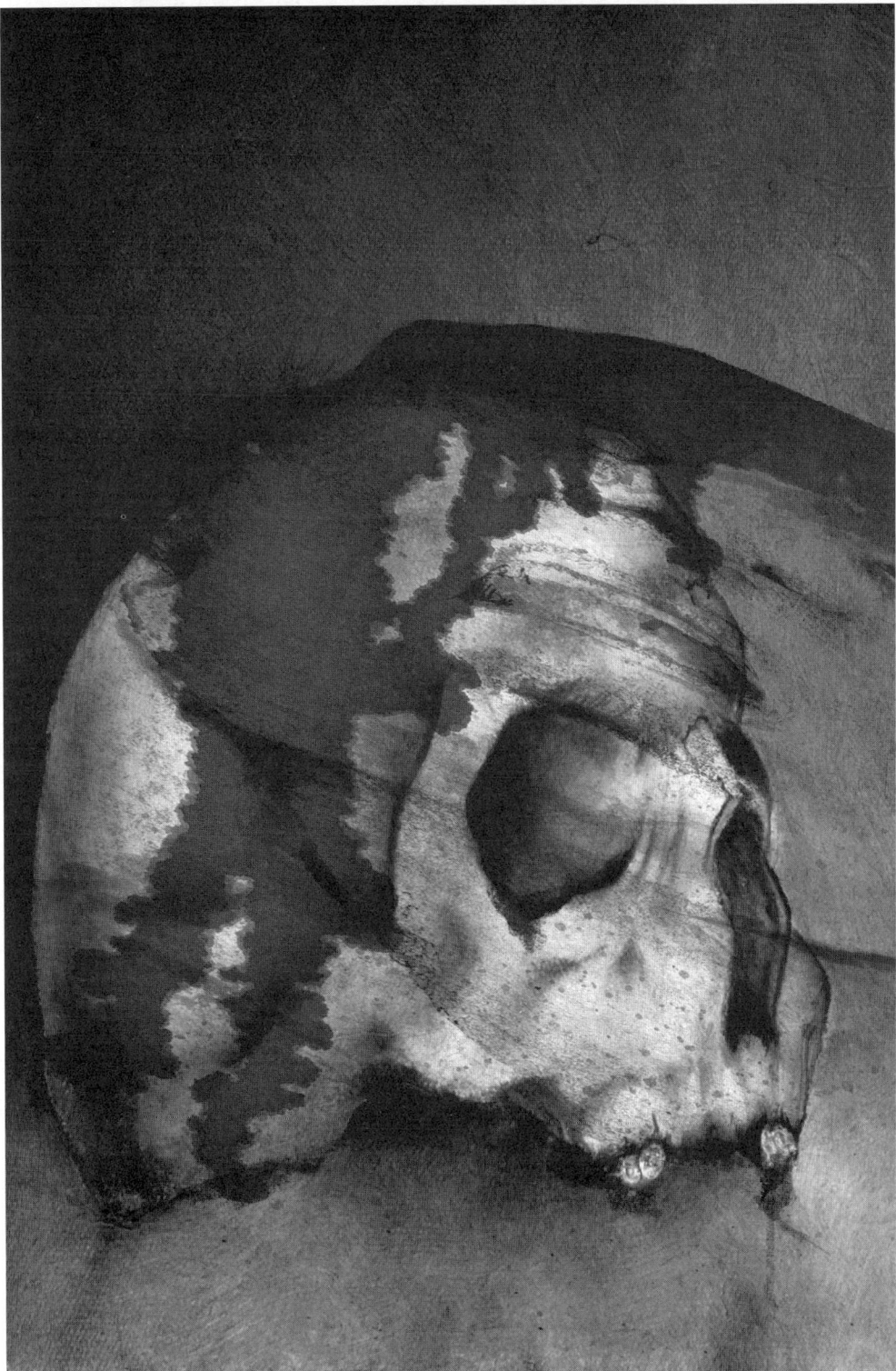

He advances toward me with the rifle pointing dangerously in my direction. As he walks, however, he stretches his arms out to hand the gun to me.

"Here you are." His eyes are terrified. "Take this. Go use it on Venus."

This takes me by surprise. "You want me to shoot your own sister?"

"You've got to."

"If you hate her so much why don't *you* blow her head off? Why ask me?"

His lips twitch. "Because I can't use it."

"You're a genius film director. You shouldn't have any trouble in figuring a gun out. You point it, then yank the trigger."

"I can't...here."

He pushes the gun at me. It seems a wise idea to take it before he attempts an experimental tug or two on the trigger.

In a spray of saliva he spits out these words: "Now kill her. Please. Before it's too late."

I check the safety's on before lowering the rifle, so its muzzle's pointing down at the earth. "Christopher." I speak matter-of-factly. "It's about your film again, isn't it? Last night you told me to destroy it before she could use it."

"Yes."

"She told me how the film works. That *Vorada* is all about this thing she calls creative destruction."

He nods. The agitation is becoming more pronounced. I realize he's frightened of us being discovered here. Little Sis terrifies him.

"Does this film brainwash people?" I ask. "Is that how it works? Subliminal images or something?"

He rushes the words out, "It does what great film does. It manipulates the viewer's thoughts and emotions. Go see—go see D.W. Griffith's *The Birth of a Nation*, or Riefenstahl's *Triumph of the Will*...their message is evil—but for a moment as you watch you'll be captured by the filmmaker's art. For a few seconds they will have brainwashed you...*yes, yes, yes!* Brainwashed you into believing their message. It doesn't matter how wrong, or how downright evil. Once the filmmaker's inside your head you believe." The speech leaves him breathless.

SHE LOVES MONSTERS

"For someone who hasn't spoken in years you're doing a fine job," I tell him.

"Venus told you I'm insane and that I never say anything." He shoots a nervous glance through the trees in the direction of the house. "That's what she tells everyone. OK, Calner. I had a breakdown. That's true, I did. Because I knew what I'd created could result in murder. People would see the film, and it would implant in their mind a suggestion. An—an irresistible suggestion that the world would be a better place if you created a martyr. Imagine if you are Catholic—a devout Catholic—you figure out for yourself that if you kill the Pope you won't destroy the Church, will you? You will have created a saint. You will make the Catholic Church more powerful and more influential."

"Wait a minute...this film is about killing the Pope?"

"No, you idiot! Its theme is about elevating a human being into that magical, powerful, wonderful creature known as a martyr. A martyr becomes immortal. A martyr is more than human. They're like a god. People will commit extraordinary acts in their name. Listen...my film will make ordinary people draw the inescapable conclusion that they will be helping humankind by killing another fellow human being that they respect." He wags his finger. *To kill an individual in power that they respect.* Not hate. That is the crucial element. Kill a good man or woman, not a dictator." He steps back, moving away all the time as he speaks. "*Vorada.* See it and you'll understand. You'll realize that to motivate humanity to find a cure for AIDS, or to rid the world of famine, or make your nation greater you must murder the Secretary-General of the UN, or the Pope, or the Dalai Lama, or the President. You'll yearn...are you listening? You will yearn to sacrifice your life and reputation in order to create something much greater. A martyr who humanity will rally around. Who will empower them. Who will make your people greater tomorrow than they are today." His eyes are blazing. He's energized by his words. "But you're smart enough to understand the human cost, aren't you?" His eyes blaze. "*Aren't you?*"

The lights are bright here in the glade. The drug reconfigures my senses. The trees are the epitome of tree-hood. Greens are the greenest. The universe is revealed. Its truths are like Russian dolls. You know the sort; those toys shaped the same as bowling pins. They have faces that reveal their inexplicable contentment at containing a series of smaller replicas secreted within them. And so life's truths are concealed one within the other. You learn one, and then find there is another truth deeper inside. These revelations spin lazily through my mind. I'm feeling it…a sense of wonder…

Christopher Lake is thirty paces away when he calls out, "You know what you've got to do, Calner. Use that gun on my sister. Then destroy the film… BURN IT!" With that he runs back to the house.

Fourteen

I find myself walking across the lawn in the direction of Montage. With this stuff flowing in my brain the architecture is even more extravagant—and exaggerated. The green bronze dome appears larger than before, minarets tower above the garden. Battlement walls are threatening to become dragon teeth that will savage lumps out of the sky. Has there been an interval between Christopher Lake's demand that I kill his sister? Or was it just seconds ago? Because the drug that's working inside of me distorts my perception of time, too. After he'd left me there in the glade with the rifle in my hands I might have stood there for ten minutes or even an hour. I was processing what Venus had told me in the gully. That tantalizing offer of hers. *"I'll give you* Vorada... *You can have whatever else you want, too."* Then I needed to digest Christopher's revelation. Did I believe this film had the power to persuade people to assassinate a president, or some great, iconic human being for the betterment of humanity? It's the drug. But the segment of my mind that makes judgments on issues such as these stands outside its usual framework. The narcotic has tinkered with my mental apparatus...and tinkered spectacularly. Greens are greener. Triangles are no longer limited to three sides. Fact is malleable.

By now I'm moving toward the house to find Venus. And you know something? The rifle feels good in my hands. The same sensation as slipping into a hand-stitched suit. It notches up the personal power quotient. The great unwashed are going to show you respect. A man with a gun walks differently to one unarmed. The body language sings a different song. *Come on, let's rip it up.*

SHE LOVES MONSTERS

Through the evening sunlight I see Bunny ambling toward me. The red light reflects in his glasses; it even lends ruby tints to his silver hair. He's carrying the scythe; its blade is stained green with nettle juice. The man who slaughtered his own parents must notice I have the rifle but gives no indication he's seen it, or, come to that, isn't remotely concerned that I should be carrying a firearm.

He smiles. It's not the beaming I'm-so-gloriously-joyful-about-life grin of old; it's a more subtle, knowing smile.

When we're ten paces apart he says to me, "She loves monsters."

"Do you consider yourself a monster?"

Bunny's smile widens. "I'm no monster. Society said I was."

"That was a monstrous act, Bunny. To kill your mother and father then burn them in their own home."

"It was a terrible decision to make, Mr. Calner. But if I hadn't, the country would have been devastated by plague."

Self-delusion. That's a drug, too. It's the most potent mind medicine of all. This white-haired man has been high on self-delusion for years.

"You said, she loves monsters. Does Venus love you?"

I watch him carefully as he makes his reply, because just asking Bunny that question twists my stomach with jealousy.

"She loves me with the same conviction as she loves the rest of humanity," he replies. "Venus Lake is blessed with a mission, Mr. Calner. Before she leaves this life she is determined to help humanity take a step forward."

"So what do you think of Venus Lake, Bunny? Monster or saint?" Without waiting to hear his reply I rest the rifle across my shoulder and continue my walk to the house. It's time to confront her—this woman: she "who loves monsters."

Fifteen

I encounter Venus Lake in the hallway. She wears a silk gown, something like a black Japanese kimono with a pattern of silver infinity symbols. Circles within circles within circles. She's brushed her brown hair. Her eyes watch my face in that interested way, which suggests the woman wants something from me. She's endeavoring to read my expression for clues that will reveal if her wishes are to be granted.

"So, Jack?" Her dark eyes flit across my face. "Are you here to kill me?"

"That wouldn't be polite, would it?" I feel a smile curl my lip. "Murder my hostess?" I click my tongue. "It just isn't done. Besides…" I fix my gaze on hers. "When you were firing this gun this morning you weren't aiming to hit me, were you?"

"So, you have been talking to my brother."

"And, despite the little white lies you've been spinning me, your brother is capable of being vocal."

"For you only, and no-one else."

"When you were blasting those bits of rock near my head this morning, and leaving that shotgun where I'd find it, you were testing me. Why?"

"You're going to be dealing with the business side of distributing and marketing Christopher's film. I needed to know if you have a killer instinct."

"And do I?"

"You fired the shotgun straight at me. If I hadn't loaded it with blanks I'd be dead now."

SHE LOVES MONSTERS

"So you needed to know that deep down I really am a monster?" I keep my eyes locked on hers. "Am I monster?"

"If a human monster can be defined as someone who is prepared to take whatever action is necessary without a conscience."

"I'm impressed, Venus." And *no way* am I being sarcastic. I AM IMPRESSED. Write it LARGE, say it **OUT LOUD**. "Truly, I'm impressed. No one's ever gone to such lengths to test me to the breaking point. You're a remarkable woman." My voice softens on the last sentence. She picks up on the change in tone from business-like to something like intimacy.

"Thank you, Jack. After the way you showed me your heart this morning I know you're a remarkable man."

"I showed you my heart as a *target*, don't forget."

There's a moment where we're communicating by glances and body language alone. That's the province of two people who are either going to fight each other or become lovers. Either way. The realization excites me.

Her smile now is a warm one. "Jack. If you don't intend using the rifle on me, then perhaps you'd like to step into the lounge. I have something to show you."

I follow her through the doorway to find her brother there. He's sitting slumped down on a sofa. His arms hang limp across his legs. For all the world, he resembles a teenager deep in a sulk. Head down, chin almost resting on his chest, he stares with unflinching resentment at the floor. *Did your sister scold you, then? Who's been a naughty boy?* Those thoughts flick through my head. I find myself shooting her a smile then glancing at Christopher as if to say, 'Just look at old grumpy boots.'

A similar glance from Venus would confirm that we are becoming allies. Before she can respond, however, Christopher's head snaps up. "You've got the rifle, Calner. Do it while you can."

"You don't really believe I'm going to blow holes in your sister?"

"More's the pity, Calner!" He spits the words. "There's not only you who'll regret it if you don't."

"The film again?" I rest the stock of the rifle on the floor and hold the muzzle in one hand. "*Vorada*." I glance from one to the other. They are more alike than I thought. Two sets of eyes beneath dark archways of eyebrows burn at me with an unusual intensity. Viper eyes, I find myself thinking. They do not blink. "You've both explained to me about *Vorada*…that just like a computer virus invades a hard drive to reprogram software so…this film will reprogram an individual's mind. That it'll compel them to assassinate a President, or strangle the Pope, or bump off a Prime Minister." I know I'm smiling. That smile makes their glare even chillier. "The biggest danger here is that the audience who sees *Vorada* will amble away to bars and restaurants afterward saying to one another, 'Wow. That was a great film. Wonderful lighting. Brilliant camera angles. Dazzling editing. Consummate production values…' all that movie-speak—jabber, jabber, jabber. But are they going to be infected by this burning need to go out and change the world by creating a martyr? Or…and, yes, this might be hard for you both to take…or will they just acknowledge that it's entertainment, and nothing more?"

"That," Venus admits, "is in the laps of the gods. We won't know how effective it is until you do your job, and make sure that when it's distributed it'll eventually reach every cinema in the Western world."

"See?" Christopher clenches his fists. "You know what she plans to do with it, Calner. In her hands it's a weapon that will—"

"Chrissie, shut up!" she snaps. "You intended the film to have this result EXACTLY. You told me it was your God-given opportunity to make the world a better place."

"But could it result in a war?" Anguish twists his features. "How could anyone predict the film's effects?"

"Creative destruction. You can't make an omelet without breaking eggs."

"Damn it, Venus! Millions could wind up dead."

I break in, "Millions? We are talking about a bit of filmed drama here. Not nuclear bombs."

Christopher's suddenly on his feet. "Why do you think I had that breakdown! I screened the entire film to some of my crew. They came to me in the days afterward and said they couldn't get this notion out of their heads that they wanted to create a martyr; they were obsessed by the idea. That's all they could think about. They said it all made such perfect sense! If they could only murder someone loved enough by the public, then the world would be a better place."

I'm angry with him, so I bark back, "Okay! So you show this to an audience of a hundred people. Ten of those become 'infected,' as you put it. They're infected by the film's message. They become obsessed by a compulsion to kill the President. But how the hell is some kid from Acacia Avenue going to put a bomb under the president's bed? Even if they get hold of a machine gun they'll never get anywhere near the president with all the security and armor plated cars. They'll just be another maniac with a gun and a one way ticket to the nut house."

"You never understand what I tell you, do you?" Saliva sprays from Lake's mouth with the force of his passion. "But you're right about one thing: *Vorada* won't affect everyone. Not everyone will read between the lines and understand its subtext: that is, to create a martyr will advance us toward social utopia; or it'll lead to a quantum leap in technology; or inspire scientists with the passion to work flat out to develop a cure for cancer. We're talking about one percent of its audience that are smart enough to draw their own conclusions."

Now Venus steps in as if suddenly she's on her brother's side. "And you have to ask yourself who will be in the audience. This is a film that anyone with a passing interest in cult cinema has been waiting to see. Just imagine for a moment, Jack." Her voice becomes silky as those fawn-soft eyes hold me. "Imagine when the film is playing in Washington D.C. where there's a member of the Secret Service, a bodyguard, or a marksman assigned to providing that security umbrella for the President. Those security servicemen are selected for their intelligence and integrity, as well as their complete and utter commitment to safeguarding the president. Before they see the film they can't think of a higher purpose in their life. They are instrumental in protecting the most powerful individual on the planet. In the battle between good and evil they are prepared to sacrifice their life. That is their purpose. Now imagine if the film suggests to them a *higher* purpose. That they can personally raise their fellow human beings to a new plateau of greater happiness. That it is in their power to endow a renewed sense of security, and reap a harvest of increased national prosperity. And that they come to believe they can achieve all this by creating a martyr who will be revered throughout history. For a personal bodyguard in an opportune location it will only take a moment." Venus's smile lights up the room. "Whoever makes the martyr doesn't even have to be armed. After all, the Emperor Romanus was drowned in his bath by his own aides."

I watch her face. Whatever she introduced to my food hasn't left me yet. Her smile illuminates my world. Even her words are blossoms of the most intense color imaginable. They're unfurling one after another inside my head.

Christopher takes a step toward me; he's pleading. "Calner. You can see what the film did to me. As soon as I understood its power I knew I could never let it go into the world. The pressure of that knowledge tore me apart."

"So why didn't you destroy it?"

"It was too late. I couldn't make that decision. My willpower was all gone. I was a wreck. It was like a paralysis of not just body but my mind, too. All I could do was lock myself away here with the film, and then pretend to your father that I was still working on it to make it perfect." He gulps as if the words have swollen in his throat so much he can barely get them out. "Your father had faith in me. He trusted me to finish the film. I wanted...I didn't know if..." As his voice ends in a croak he turns away. He's rubbing his temples as if the pressure inside is so great he fears it will erupt through the bone. As for me? I'm in the grip of the chemicals in my blood again. Maybe this is its last psychedelic surge of mind-altering magic.

"Jack?" Venus smiles that smile of pure honey for my soul. She grips my forearm in both her hands. I feel her body press up close to mine. "We're nearly there, aren't we? Doesn't it feel as if we're just a step away from something marvelous?"

Christopher's haggard eyes fix on me. "You've got the rifle, Mr. Calner. You only have to stick it in her face and pull the trigger. You'll save the world so much heartache if you do. What's the use of a martyr anyway?"

The setting sun floods the room with red light. Suddenly it seems as if the walls are drenched in blood. Crimson is splashed on those marble statues of Greek gods and goddesses. Apollo's face has the appearance of being carved from raw beef.

It's that little pill that Venus melted into my soup, I tell myself. It hasn't stopped casting its spell yet.

"Calner." Christopher Lake speaks through gritted teeth. "You must stop Venus. This could be your last chance." He punches down on the table. "Kill her!"

SHE LOVES MONSTERS

Venus snaps, "Save your breath, Chrissie. Can't you see? Jack won't be using that gun on me." She rests those slender fingers on my arm again, "You could never hurt me, could you, Jack?"

I shake my head. A solemn shake. This provokes the man to act. With a howl he snatches a glass figurine from the table top. I see it happening. I know what he will do with it. But this drug has put me in a place outside myself. It's as if I'm watching all this happen to a stranger...not to me. So there's no burning need to react.

Venus shouts. I track the sweep of his arm with my eyes. The foot-tall statue of a Greek huntress glitters with cranberry lights in the setting sun. I feel nothing but tranquil detachment. At some point during this swirl of movement Lake dashes the figurine into my forehead. There's no pain but I'm falling back onto the floor. Venus is there, helping me to my feet. Once more I'm impressed by the understanding that I can't tell how much time has passed between being clubbed by the glass figurine and a slow motion rise to my feet with Venus's anxious face looking into mine. As I stand I realize that the automatic rifle is no longer in my hands; it has made the short but crucial journey into those of Christopher—he of cracked mind. These are the thoughts that are surprising, yet expected, surreally funny yet simultaneously alarming. That blow he delivered to my skull was harder than I thought. Venus is having to exert herself to keep me upright.

Christopher Lake backs away until he's a dozen paces from us. The combination of the drug and the crack across the head with the figurine leaves me detached. I see all this happening as if I'm perched high in the minstrel's gallery at the end of the lounge. I'm standing there, supported by Venus in her rippling silk kimono. Her lunatic brother is fumbling with the automatic rifle. His movements are fast. To my mind they're exaggerated as his fingers pull at levers on the rifle. He's trying to find the safety catch. I know he is. Because he's tugged at the trigger at least five times without successfully firing the rifle.

And Venus is shouting, "No, Christopher. Put the gun down...listen to me, put it down!"

I'm saying nothing. I seem to have more in common with those marble statues. Right at that moment a stone-like quality is preferable to anything of flesh and feeling.

"Christopher...Chrissie, please. Don't do this. Put the gun on the table, then go back to your room. I'll bring supper. You can listen to your music…"

"Venus…I'm not an imbecile. I'm going to stop you." The clouded expression of confusion on the man's face suddenly brightens into one of wonder as at last he manages to slide the safety catch into fire mode.

My senses return in a rush. The mental image of Venus and I being torn to pieces by high-velocity ammunition hits me with brutal force. "You won't do this, Christopher. Give me the rifle."

The expression of wonder that appeared on his face as he realized he had a killing machine in his hands evolves into one of grim determination. "I'm sorry. But you know why I've got to kill her. You know what she's planning? She's wanting to set the world on fire. Creative destruction? It'd lead to nothing but pure destruction. There'd be utter carnage." Lake swings the rifle muzzle to point it at her. He holds it awkwardly; he's not familiar with firearms. I know, however, that at this range he can not miss. Venus stiffens as she realizes he really does intend to open fire.

The blast comes like a roar of thunder. Venus flinches. Her body snaps against mine. I search her face for an expression of agony. With all my will-power I pray she won't die. Yet, as my eyes fix on her, I realize she's turning to stare at her brother. I glance back to see him lurching backward with his arms outstretched. The rifle tumbles from his hands to the floor. A second later his body slaps down onto the mosaic. There he lies. On his back, with his arms flung outward. Blood trickles from his mouth. More of the stuff seeps through his shirt in a crimson mass that engulfs the entire area of his chest.

That gust of pure fear has flushed the drug right out of me. I'm ME again. Jack Calner. I'm clear headed. The world is as it always has been. Colors and perspectives are normal. I still have my arm around Venus' shoulders as I glance back to see Bunny standing in the doorway. He holds the shotgun to his shoulder; it's still aimed at the few cubic feet of air that, until a moment ago, were occupied by one deranged filmmaker by the name of Christopher Lake. Auteur of long lost *Vorada*. Blue smoke oozes from the muzzle of the gun. Whereas moments ago the room had been filled with what seemed like an explosion, along with a shriek of lead pellets tearing the air, and the impact of Lake against the floor—all of those rolled into one avalanche of sound—now there is profound silence.

SHE LOVES MONSTERS

Forty years after Bunny murdered his parents he's gone and killed all over again.

For a while, the tableau remains just like that. I stand with my arms around Venus. Bunny poses, motionless, in the doorway with the shotgun, his eyes locked onto his victim. Christopher Lake lies dead on the floor.

Despite the powerful smells of spilt body fluids and cordite, I'm noticing other things now. The song of birds in the evening sunlight reaches me through the open window. I can smell stinging nettles again.

It seems to touch Bunny, too, who relaxes with a sigh. He lowers the shotgun so it dangles harmlessly in one hand with its muzzle pointing down at the floor.

"Miss Lake." His smile returns, yet this time it's sympathetic. "I'm sorry I had to do that to your brother. I know how much you loved him."

She takes a deep breath to steady herself. "You did the right thing, Bunny."

"I'll wait until the end of the week. Then I'll report what I've done to the police."

She nods. "Thank you. That'll give us time to announce to the press about the release of the film before my brother's death becomes public knowledge."

I feel as if I'm having to run hard to keep up with the thread of this conversation.

"Venus. Bunny has just killed your brother. You need to—"

"I need to put my plan into action first, that's what I need to do, Jack." She steps forward to gaze down at the corpse then glances back at me. "And don't stare at me like that. I'm not a heartless bitch. We need to collect the film then get it to the distributors as quickly as possible. When news of Christopher's death breaks there'll be plenty of publicity we can use."

"And I thought *I* was ruthless."

Suddenly she's business-like again. "You'll get what you want, Jack. Money, lots of money; more than you can ever spend. And I'll get…" Her voice fades as she fully appreciates the enormity of events.

I finish her sentence. "You'll get your martyr." I glance at Bunny who smiles at her, and then I turn back to Venus. "You really do love monsters." I can't resist saying this. Talk about bad timing and insensitivity, but... "Bunny killed his parents to stop a plague from wiping us out. Now he's killed Christopher, who planned to stop you from releasing his film. *Vorada's* going to create your martyr, and that martyr will elevate this world to a better place."

I address Bunny. "It's becoming quite a habit. You've saved humanity all over again. Well done." A sarcastic note adds a sour tone to my voice. Bunny doesn't notice. Or he doesn't give a damn. Either way, his heart will be bursting with heroic pride.

Venus locks those big brown eyes on me. "Jack. We're both going to get what we want from this film. So you're not going to try and stop me—are you?"

Sixteen

Now it is dark.

Expedient. This word can sting the conscience like those stinging nettles we cut earlier can prickle your skin. Expediency isn't for the weak. Many a time in the past I've done what is expedient—or necessary, if you prefer that word—with a reasoned and considered disregard for morality. I'm a businessman, after all.

Now this is expedient. In its own way it's moving, too, just in case you think I've a heart beaten from solid brass. In the hour since Christopher Lake was shot dead in the living room here at Montage I watched this happen.

Refusing help from either Venus or myself, Bunny carried Christopher's body upstairs to his bedroom. With tenderness, love and utter respect, this white haired man who'd murdered his mother and father half a lifetime ago sets Christopher on his bed. Venus follows them into the room. She presses a button on the laptop. The applause recorded in a Parisian concert hall fills the room. It's followed by the eerie notes of an accordion, and once more Jacques Brel thunders his hymn to sailors carousing in the Port of Amsterdam against a back drop of the eternal. From the foot of the bed, she watches as Bunny adjusts her dead brother's limbs until it appears he lies there dozing, not dead. He makes a beautiful corpse. There, I've said it. It's a strange observation, yet true. Christopher Lake could be posing for a painting of a fallen warrior.

It's tranquil in the house now. There's no panic. Everyone moves in an unrushed way. Our voices are relaxed; no-one speaks loudly. I pack

SHE LOVES MONSTERS

my clothes and put the bag in the car. The night is still. A new moon shines down. Lights burn inside Montage. Through its open windows drifts the sound of the male voice singing in French. The mood of the song is tidal. At times it creeps along in a somber, melancholy way before surging upward in floods of triumph. Venus told me it's a song about a sailor drinking hard, getting into a brawl, and then dying in a dockside bar. At that moment, as the music pours out over the moonlit garden, it becomes a rhapsody to life's conquest of death.

Then I'm back in the house again. Bunny is mopping blood from the mosaic dolphins in the living room. Venus Lake sits on her brother's bed. She's holding his hands while she gazes at his face in genuine sorrow. The music's still playing, but quietly now.

"When we were young," she begins, "we'd build sandcastles. Then we'd pretend that we gathered all the frightened and vulnerable people in the world together, and then put them in the castle. Christopher would tell me it was the strongest castle there ever was, and now the people inside would be safe. No-one would ever be able to hurt them again. When he grew up his films became his sandcastle. *Vorada* was going to be the biggest and the best. But he lost his nerve." She stands then gently kisses him on the forehead. "Goodbye, Christopher."

Seventeen

We're driving away from Montage. Even though the sound of Jacques Brel's music fades from my ears I can still hear it play on inside my head. Venus sits beside me. Of course, I haven't had a chance to have the cracked windshield replaced. Venus Lake's naked body shattered that glass. I marvel over this fact more than once as I watch the road through the crazed pattern of white lines. But then she has constantly surprised me from that first encounter with her when she raced from the forest to smash into the front of my car. When I first spoke to her she appeared naiveté, but I realize now that she was simply wearing that naivety as a disguise. In all of this she's been in control. The car's headlights slice through the darkness in front of us. At that moment there's also the searing beam of insight cutting through the inside of my head—my still aching head. I mean, just look at what Venus Lake has done:

Naked, she ran into my car. An accident? Now I wonder.

Duped me into thinking she was a simple woman of limited intelligence.

Enticed me into desiring her…no, it's more powerful than that. Venus Lake succeeded in making me fall in love with her.

She made me scuttle around that woodland folly like a frightened rabbit as she fired off the rifle.

She put drugs in my soup. Just like I swallowed everything she told me I swallowed those, too.

After that, she lured me out of the house to chase her as she ran naked through the trees.

SHE LOVES MONSTERS

Then, when my mind had been turned inside out by the narcotic, she tells me that *Vorada* will radically alter the civilized world. And this is the method: Its story-line will suggest to certain individuals that progress—both social and technological—is accelerated either by a world war, or by the death of a public figure beloved by all, who will become a martyr in the eyes of the masses. With me so far? Good.

Because now I feel a tingle down my spine. Understand this, Venus is exceptional. She calculates her actions will achieve the results she wants. If everything she has done since her brother completed *Vorada* has been a logical step-by-step process in her quest to change the world, then—listen to me carefully now—then I must reach a conclusion that the film will successfully complete her meticulous strategy. Venus will create her martyr. The world will change.

These thoughts loop round and round in my head as I drive. It's near to midnight now as the car surges along the forest highway. It'll take around six hours to reach my house in London. For a while, we've been chatting in a friendly way. If I'm reading the signals right she'll be giving me more than reels of film. In a matter of hours we'll be sharing a bed. The images that spin in my mind quicken my pulse. I want her. That's the long and the short of it. I want her so much I ache. And it's one of those absurd universal truths of life that most men are prepared to undertake a heck of a lot of uncharacteristic activity if there's a chance of sexual intercourse at the end of it. Such as serenading their heart's desire with a guitar beneath her window; or writing long love letters; or driving cross-country to make that all-important rendezvous; or…in my case… yes, in my case, doing everything in my power to make sure that the film her brother—now lying bloody and dead in his bedroom—made all those years ago will finally be released to a worldwide audience. That's it, isn't it? I'm doing this for love…puppy-eyed, head-over-heels, madly-truly-deeply, forever-and-ever-without-end kind of love…

Thoughts like these, and their piggy-back images of sizzling erotic sex, push me to drive faster. I power the car along the road; its lights splash against bushes and trees. The moon is high above the hills.

After what we've been through together over the last forty-eight hours I'm sure she'll confide in me now.

"So," I begin as I accelerate out of a bend, "now you can tell me where you hid the film."

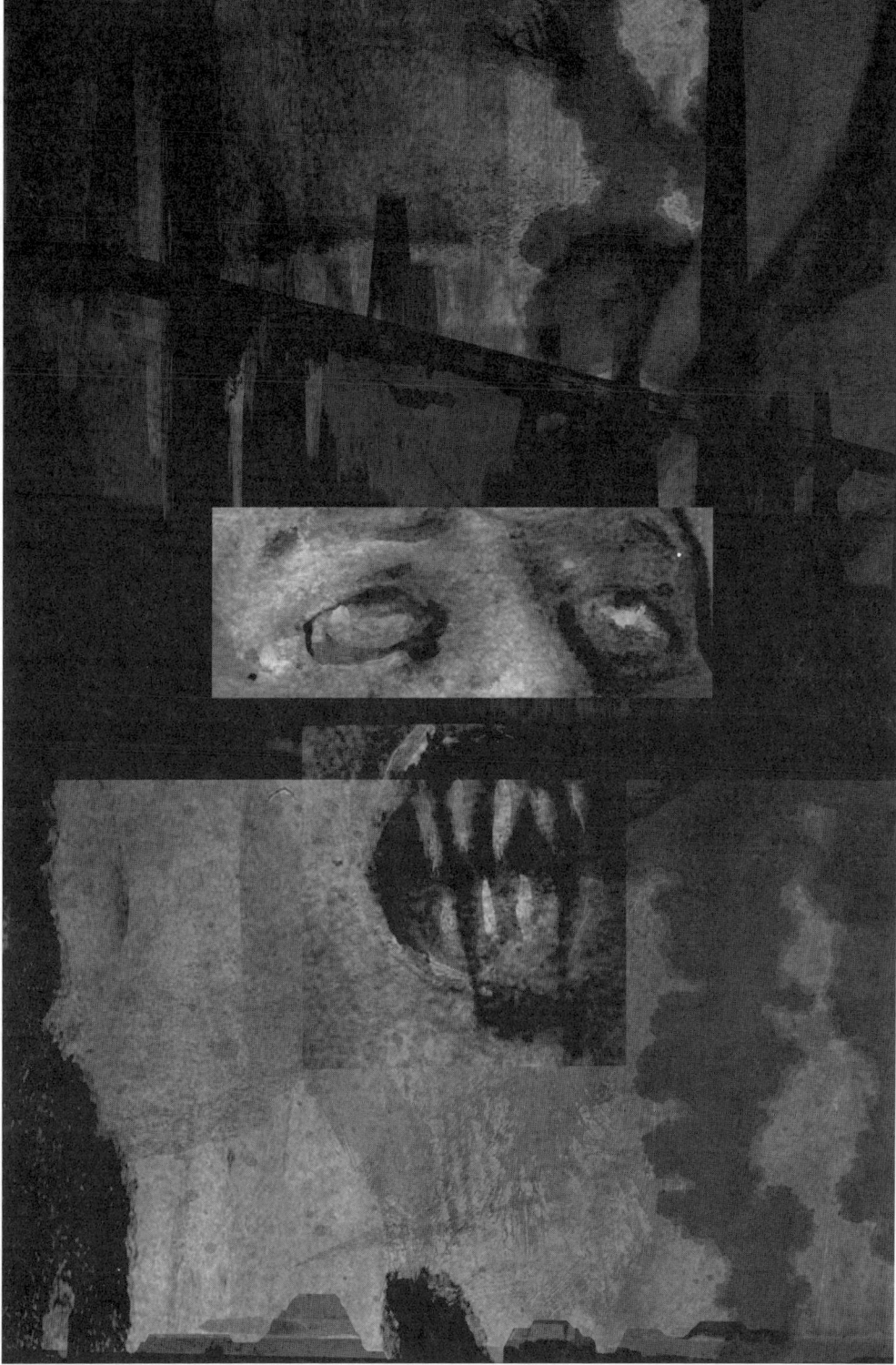

Venus looks at me without answering. There's a Mona Lisa smile ghosting on her lips.

I continue: "It can't be back at the house, can it?"

"I know better than to leave thousands of feet of priceless celluloid lying around in a garage or an attic. Years ago I took it to a safety deposit vault. It was secure; the temperature and humidity were controlled. It's cost a hell of a lot to keep it there, but…" She shrugs as if the end of the sentence is obvious.

I agree. "Something that valuable deserves the best."

She nods.

"So when do we collect?" I ask.

Her smile broadens. "This is the plan. I'll arrange a press call at a hotel in London. You'll read a speech I've prepared, which talks about cult director Christopher Lake, the history of *Vorada* and your plans for its release. I'll collect the film, and for dramatic effect I'll wheel it in for the media to photograph and no doubt carry its reappearance live on news channels the world over. At the press conference I hand the reels over to the distributor who will take it away, and make the necessary copies. At the same time you take care of the business side. Promotion, marketing, rights deals and so on."

"You've got this all covered." On the road ahead rabbits scatter in the car's lights. They avoid death by inches. "But what about the fact Bunny killed your brother?"

"It's a tragedy I didn't foresee. Until tonight Chrissie was never violent. Anyway, we can't turn back time. Bunny knows what I plan to do, and that we need a couple of days to get everything in place before he goes to the police. Bunny won't implicate us. He'll confess to shooting Christopher after we'd left for London."

"And as he's murdered before the police are unlikely to doubt Bunny's confession." I nod. "Does Bunny know where the film is?"

"No. Only I do."

"You won't share its location with me, Venus?"

"There's no need at this stage."

"You've really got this all planned to the letter, haven't you?"

"Yes. Because it's the most important thing I've ever done in my life." Her face is illuminated by the dashboard lights. "You've never had a conviction that you were born in order to fulfill a destiny, Jack?"

SHE LOVES MONSTERS

"I've had ambition for personal gain. Never destiny." In her face I can see that single purpose in her life. It shines there. It's unquenchable. Nothing else matters. If she has to sacrifice her own life to make sure that *Vorada* gets seen by even more people then she'll do it.

It's been an extraordinary forty-eight hours. When I first drove through this forest toward Montage I wouldn't have believed the film I was hunting had the power to change the civilized world. Christopher Lake even said it might trigger new wars. I wouldn't have believed any of that—not for one, lousy moment—but this woman beside me has the power to work a new kind of magic. It's a magic that has the power to transfigure minds. Without a scrap of doubt I know the film will achieve everything she claims. Oh, it'll make me even wealthier in the process. Even if it does cost the life of one famous, iconic human being. Go on, read your history books. Martyrs change the world. Although there is a risk that such an assassination might lead to the deaths of thousands of men, women and children. I guess that's what they term "collateral damage."

And so... Venus Lake asks if I've ever had a sense of my own destiny. This has provoked a whole slew of disparate thoughts. I recall Christopher Lake's pleas to stop this. I'm struck that I never even asked what *Vorada* was about. Brel's song is in my head. Life beats death. Ultimately, it always does. Maybe at this precise second I'm not thinking clearly. It occurs to me that my brain isn't clear of the drug after all. And even now it's shaping the way I think. Maybe this isn't noble at all. That the sense of shared destiny that fills me at this instant might be nothing more than another chemical-induced hallucination.

But, God help me, *this* seems to be the right decision.

As I press the pedal to the floor and the car hurtles along this wilderness road I close my eyes. I keep them closed. I keep them tightly shut even as Venus Lake shouts my name and tries to grab the wheel.

I keep them closed... I'm keeping them closed... I'm keeping—

"Jack! I know what you're doing. It won't work!"

The car leaves the road. For now, there are no obstructions. It rolls in the air.

Venus speaks. There's no fear. Only the pure note of destiny that resonates. "Jack. I lied. Bunny knows where *Vorada*—"

94. EXT. FOREST - DAY

Seasons change. Summer has gone. Now winter blows in. Trees are bare. It's a monochrome landscape of black trees and white snow on the ground. Deep in a gully out of sight from the world is JACK CALNER'S silver BMW. Its bodywork is crumpled, the windshield missing; vines climb over the roof. Strapped in the front seats are the two decomposing corpses of VENUS and JACK. FADE IN APPLAUSE and CALLS from an audience as Brel's AMSTERDAM begins. Ghostly notes of the ACCORDION rise in volume. UNASSIGNED CAMERA of car, rocks and trees as if POV is becoming detached from the tragedy that unfolded here ten months ago. CAMERA drifts away from the car to wander through the frozen forest in search of other lives.

«« — »»

FOUR MONTHS LATER

From: THE LEEDS BRIDGE REVIEW #177
Writer/Director: Christopher Lake
Running Time: 190 minutes
Released: OUT NOW!

Enough said. This is what you, me and the kids from UCLA have been waiting for. The famous lost *Vorada* of Lake's that, legend has it, cost more lives than the construction of the Hoover Dam. Go now! See it! All one-hundred and ninety numinous minutes of Lake's *über* vision. Then stay up all night arguing about its hidden meaning…

«« — »»

From: NEWS EUROPE
"So this is the commencement of novemdiales, the nine days of official mourning ordered by the Vatican for a man whose life was taken by those he trusted most."

«« — »»

SHE LOVES MONSTERS

From: WASHINGTON, D.C. POLICE DEPARTMENT
Transcript of the first 911 call:
"This is a confession… I'm sorry… I've just killed him…"

Midword

Or A Message From The Borderland

Boundaries? Malleable, plastic, flexible, shifting, stretchy, elastic. Here today, gone tomorrow.

Borders? Permeable, porous, leaky, breakable, breachable. Neither here nor there.

Barriers? What barriers? There are no barriers.

For a long time, perhaps since early childhood, I've had this abiding fascination where two areas that should be distinct and completely separate behave just the opposite. An idea I find compelling is where two distinct territories have a tendency—or even an irresistible compulsion—to hemorrhage into one another. The states of life and death are perfect examples. In the latter the border between the two should be unbreachable. Although what is living might become dead, what is dead SHOULD NEVER *EVER* become living.

But that's where the horror writer gleefully breaks the rule. He or she tears down the barrier between death and life. And before you know it the dead can walk that path toward the living. Mummies, vampires, zombies, ghosts—in the horror writer's imagination here they come to intrude on the men and women who are still in the pink. Other barriers that should be sacrosanct can easily be demolished by imagination, too. The past is a world beyond our reach. Until, that is, fiction works its magic; then in a time-travel story we can bring Hitler onto New York's Broadway of 2006, and have him explore a world where history so rightly judges him as one of the most evil men whoever lived. Or we can focus on you—yes *you*, reading these words right now. In my next novella you fall asleep in your chair only to wake in the year 3838. You hurry outside to find the world has become…

SHE LOVES MONSTERS

Well, that's another story. What I'm driving at here is that I have a thing about boundaries—a real THING-AND-A-HALF. Boundaries are an irritant. I long to get my fingernails into them and scratch them away. Then I can blur the distinction between reality and fantasy. For example, grab another scenario as it glides by on wings of fancy. Here a man believes he's facing a life and death struggle on a civil war battlefield only to discover to his astonishment he's really an actor in a movie.

"I'm sure the actor would have figured out that he's playing a part in a film," Jack Calner said as he eyed the bright green soup with interest. "He'd see the lights and the camera and the director shouting 'Action.' Are you sure stinging nettles are edible?"

"Not only are they edible," Venus Lake replied as she busied herself at the kitchen stove, "they're good for you. You'd be surprised how many plants growing wild contain all kinds of healing properties."

"Huh, if I die writhing in agony I'll choke out 'I told you so' with my final breath." Jack tasted the soup. "A bit like spinach. Now, all this you were saying about boundaries and borders…you've stayed marooned out here too long in the wilderness. Trust me, the demarcation between fact and fiction is far more durable and impermeable than you imagine."

"Don't you believe it, Jack. Just because a writer types THE END, or the film maker puts up the final caption FINIS—it doesn't mean the story is really over."

"Venus, like I said, you've lived out here too long with that brother of yours and strange old Bunny the gardener."

For a moment Venus Lake's eyes became wistful as she toyed with her hair. "I remember as a girl I used to love those TV programs with deceptive endings. You know, where you thought the comedy show had ended and a serious documentary had started; only it wasn't a different program, it was still the comedy and something outrageous and unexpected would happen."

"Sit down and eat your soup," Jack told her. "It's getting cold."

"Don't you remember shows like that? *Monty Python* was always doing it. I think there might have even been an old *Twilight Zone* episode where something similar happened. Wasn't it the one starring William Shatner?"

"I don't know." Jack broke off a piece of bread to dunk in his soup. "I never watched it."

"Then you missed a treat."

"It sounds subversive to me, Venus."

"In what way subversive?"

"It manipulates you by manipulating the truth."

"At the trial of Jesus Christ didn't Pilate ask 'What is truth?'"

"Pilate wasn't being philosophical, he was being sarcastic. The trial would have been run-of-the-mill for him. He merely wanted to move onto more important matters. Probably taxation or import tariffs. Matters fiscal, anyway. You know, this is the greenest food I've ever eaten in my life. It's outrageous."

"But you do like it?" Suddenly Venus seemed eager to please.

Jack Calner inwardly glowed when he realized a beautiful woman was so eager to please him. It opened so many agreeable possibilities. He nodded but held back on too fulsome a praise. "Not bad…for stinging nettles."

She watched him. Her large, fawn-like eyes were luminous.

"Jack," she began in a gentle voice. "You never did ask what *Vorada* was about."

"Ah, your genius brother's famous lost film." He shrugged. "Does its story really matter now?"

"It was the most autobiographical film Christopher ever made. It revealed things about both of us. Especially me. When we were in our teens we—"

"Ah," Jack held up his spoon that was streaked with that emerald liquid. "There you go again. Autobiography. All autobiographies are a fantasia of subjective recollections."

"*Vorada* is the most brutally honest autobiography you'll ever see."

"'Autobiography' and 'honest' are words that shouldn't be employed in the same sentence, Venus."

She fixed Jack with those beautiful eyes. "That's not true."

"Prove it."

"Finish your soup, Jack. I can show you an autobiography later. And in a little while I'm sure you'll have a different way of looking at things."

Jack shrugged. He continued spooning the savory liquid into his

SHE LOVES MONSTERS

mouth. As he did so he heard the sound of applause come ghosting down the corridor to the kitchen where they both sat. Following that, there rose the eerie notes of an accordion played by a musician, who was probably now long dead, to an audience who would have joined him too in that little field of bones. Christopher Lake was playing Jacques Brel's haunting hymn to the phantoms of sailors drinking, dancing and carousing with women in the Port of Amsterdam long, long ago.

As the singer reached out to him across the gulf of space and time in a language Jack Calner didn't understand, he asked himself this: Does a ghost know when it is a ghost? Can humanity ever truly know what it is like to be dead? And when the blood of oblivion flies through their veins, do the dead dream that they live forever?

Jack Calner put down the spoon, and broke his bread as the reader turned the page.

One

The True Story Of The Hunt For The "One Thing."

The Ghost's Lair

"You wanna join our gang?"
"Yes."
"You're sure, Simon?"
"Yes."
"You've got to promise to do whatever we say. Got that?"
"Okay."
"Right. To be able to join our gang you've got to jump off that wall."
"That wall?"
"Yep. That wall."
"But it's ten feet high. I'll break my legs if I jump off that."
"You want to be in our gang, don't you, Simon?"
"Yes."
"Then jump off the wall."
"It's too high."

The initiation rites weren't going as I'd expected. I thought they'd ask me to touch a nettle or shout a swear word. But that wall... No way! I'd break both my legs into a hundred pieces if I jumped off that.

The stony faces of the gang members told me I wouldn't be joining their elite corps after all. I was going to be alone again. And at six years old I really did believe it was time for me to join the big boys.

One boy must have had a heart veined with gold. Although he didn't relent, he had the makings of a diplomat somewhere in his bones.

SHE LOVES MONSTERS

He looked at the wall (which they'd jumped off with ease) and thought for a moment. Then he said, "He's got short trousers on."

"What's that got to do with it?" asked another boy suspiciously.

"Well, look at that broken glass. He'd cut his knees, wouldn't he?"

"Simon Clark's got to pass a test if he's going to join our gang." The boy decided to add some meat to the argument. "We don't want a sissy going around with us."

Proto-diplomat had a solution. "Why not show him the ghost?"

Stubborn one wasn't convinced. "Why?"

"If he'd dare go see the ghost then he's brave enough for our gang."

The other gang members liked the idea. What's more, they saw that the Sunday afternoon wasn't going to be as boring as they first thought.

"Yeah," they said, grinning. "Show Simon the ghost!"

Now I was the suspicious one. "What ghost?"

"We know where there's a ghost."

"There's no such thing as ghosts," I said (but already shivers had started creeping up my spine). "They don't exist."

"This one does. And we're going to show you it."

Another boy grinned at me. "That is if you want to be in our gang?"

I nodded. And that's when they took me to the ghost's lair.

We set off through a maze of derelict houses. Some were boarded up. Some had already been demolished. It was a lonely place. A desert of pulverized brick, of broken windows that stared like dead eyes.

It was the kind of place where you could scream yourself sick and no one would even hear, let alone come running to see who—or *what*—was torturing you.

We picked our way over fallen masonry, through skeletons of long dead houses, moving from sunlight into semi-darkness, where there was the mushroom smell of damp and decay.

Normally my big sister would have been keeping an eye on me. But a girl had been murdered just a few days earlier. Now the police were interviewing some of the local children to build up a profile of the victim.

The murderer was still at large.

Soon, we reached a ruined house.

"In you go, Simon," one of the gang said, smiling.

I paused before the yawning doorway. "There really is a ghost in here?"

SIMON CLARK

The boy nodded.

I was nervous by this time. My heart beat faster and faster. There was some kind of disgusting promise contained in the rooms I glimpsed through the open doorway. Although they were empty of furniture, the rooms held a powerful sense of presence. A presence that had (if you were foolish enough to enter) the power to change you forever. I was too young to understand what such power might be. But I sensed its threat as surely as if I could see some dark, noxious beast lurking in the shadows.

The simple truth was I wanted—no, I *needed* to join that gang.

So despite my better instincts screaming NO! I walked through the door, into the cold, damp air of the hallway.

And went to meet whatever waited for me there.

Here I can pause the narrative as though it's a DVD. And there I am: Simon Clark, six years old, blue eyes, blonde hair, freckles speckling a snub nose, legs still retaining a baby-ish chubbiness, one tentative foot stepping forward, taking me from the cozy world of childhood into the "óther place"…a new world. Not adulthood, not yet, but into the borderland between childhood and being "grown-up."

I lived in a modest house with my mother (an office worker with a love of song and dance movies) and my father (a schoolteacher with a passion for sport). And then there was big sister Karen (gregarious, good-looking) and Skipper the West Highland White Terrier. Next door lived my grandparents (grandfather: dreamer, musician, local politician and city mayor; and grandmother: a kindly, timid woman who did voluntary work, and brewed mysterious herbal drinks from plants she found in hedge bottoms).

Already I was an imaginative kid, with a hunger for science fiction and fairy tales and a compulsion to make up stories. "I've got monster robots that live in the attic. I give them orders and they go out every night and get people," I'd tell my friends. They didn't believe me. At least they said they didn't but more than one of them would always run by our house while shooting scared glances up at the roof. And there was a human skull buried under the garage, or so my father told me.

In fact, the house was awash with such stories. My many uncles (teenagers at the time) were full of "true tales" about local murders, mutilations and haunted houses. I believed them all.

SHE LOVES MONSTERS

The Clarks have Nordic looks and build. A thousand years ago, Viking warriors had coaxed their longships up the black, tideless river known as the Calder to about as far inland as you can get in England. There they'd beached the boats and founded a town called Wakefield, now a bustling city. Perhaps my ancestors arrived on one of those boats. In any event the Clark family had lived in Wakefied, as the saying goes, since time immemorial.

So, there in 1964, one of who must have been a long line of Clarks was just about to encounter the unknown.

With just one touch of the mental play button the six-year-old Simon Clark is in motion once more. Stepping through the door, into the shadows, with the smell of decay slithering up my nostrils.

"Where's the ghost?" I asked, shivering to the roots of my heart.

The boys hung back in the sunlight outside. "Go to the door across from you. Open it. There's steps going down into a cellar."

I obeyed. I opened the door. Steps led down into a pit that oozed darkness.

Heart cracking against my ribs, I stepped closer and looked down. "I can't see a ghost."

"*Just wait!*" they chorused back at me.

So I waited…and I watched, my eyes fixed at the bottom of the seemingly vast number of stairs that led down to a dark, sinister and infinitely mysterious world.

Suddenly my muscles locked up tight. My neck seemed to stretch out longer and longer. Peculiar things were happening to my body. It was my first experience of physical fear, maybe even terror.

There at the bottom of the steps, moving from left to right across the cellar floor was a shape.

It was dark, humped. It possessed no head.

I didn't scream. I didn't run. I just stood there, watching.

When it had passed out of sight, I simply turned round and walked out of the derelict house. I went home without speaking a word to the others, or even acknowledging they were there. I never joined the gang.

Okay.

Maybe it was my imagination.

SIMON CLARK

Maybe it was one of the other kids with a jacket over his head to ape the headless phantom.

But the effect it had on me was profound.

Six-year-old Simon Clark believed he had seen a REAL ghost.

It might have been an experience of pure horror then but it was, in fact, the first step on the road to my career.

My Own Frankenstein

Was there a single moment when I realized I wanted to be a horror writer? Well...not exactly. The best comparison is that I was like the steel ball in a pinball machine being blasted from pin to bell. Like seeing the 'ghost,' there was a series of encounters and experiences that blasted me toward being a writer.

So:

BANG!

We moved from metropolitan Wakefield to the tiny village of Thorpe Audlin. Aged seven, I now had fields to roam in where I could allow my imagination to roam further still. I walked with my friends to woodlands at Wentbridge where Robin Hood and his men had held wrestling tournaments. When we nagged our parents into buying us air pistols, we stopped walking. We swaggered.

TRANGG!

The Apollo moonshots. I watched as much as I could. I took photographs of the TV screen to capture the moment of "That's one small step..." But all I got were prints of a blank screen and 60's TV set in an imitation wood case. It didn't matter. In my head, I was up there with the astronauts.

ZAPPP!

I went to a school with fifty pupils run by a husband-and-wife teaching team. In retrospect, I imagine they were embarking on a brave (and probably unsanctioned) educational experiment. Very little in the way of structured lessons; very little overt discipline. And a lot of time for long nature walks, and for pupils to write stories and

SHE LOVES MONSTERS

poetry, and to allow that strange and powerful creature called IMAGINATION to grow and grow and become stronger and stronger. For most kids this was at a steady and controllable rate. My imagination, on the other hand, turned into a great galumphing Frankenstein.

My Frankenstein imagination tolerated no competitors for whatever passes as nutrients that feed the human mind. My abilities in subjects such as mathematics, science, economics—any subjects that require discipline, and a capacity to endure boredom—were brutally destroyed. However, it excelled at anything that was driven by imagination, such as poetry and story writing.

BUZZZZ!

One night I listened to the radio alone in my bedroom. Lightning flashed; thunder stomped across the sky like the feet of Titans. Tuning the radio, I came across a voice booming like thunder, too. I didn't know what or who it was at the time (in fact, it was Dylan Thomas belting out *And Death Shall Have No Dominion*) but I was frightened and electrified. A defining moment.

Revelation: **I sensed the power of words.**

ZZ-FRANG!

Aged around eleven, I saw *Quatermass And The Pit* on television. A mating of ghost story with science fiction, it enthralled me. At that moment I thought: 'I want to be involved in something like that.' I didn't know whether I wanted to be a cameraman, writer, actor or director. I only wanted to be part of the machine that made mind-zapping stories such as *Quatermass* (and *Bride Of Frankenstein* and *War Of The Worlds* and *The Hunchback Of Notre Dame*).

VVRAA-ANG!

The Beast goes East. My parents took me to Greece. I all but lived in the sea for a fortnight with my mask and snorkel. I swam with shoals of fish over walls that had once been on dry land but had been submerged by earthquakes. I saw the mummified body of a saint paraded on feast days. My Frankenstein imagination feasted on all kinds of exotic stimuli. It grew bigger…stronger…

ZWAPPPP!

Age thirteen. I'd been reading heaps of Asimov, Clarke, Lovecraft and Wyndham, along with umpteen anthologies of horror stories and science fiction. It was a summer's evening. I was walking with my dog,

SIMON CLARK

Skipper, down the field toward the stream. The sound of bells came pealing across meadows from a distant church.

And quietly, but with complete certainty, I knew at that moment what I would do with my life: I would become a writer.

Into The Wilderness

A writer?

How the hell do you become a writer?

There are no apprenticeships. There were no college courses (at least none that I knew of then). In my tiny Yorkshire village of Thorpe Audlin there were no writers to advise me (or, again, at least none that I knew of). I doubted if a careers teacher could help me. At my high school, bright kids went to university. The not-so-bright went down THE PIT (a nice horror-sounding term for a career in coal mining, which was, in fact, deeply horrific, dangerous and usually resulted in premature death).

I wasn't one of the bright kids. Yes, I had my great galumphing Frankenstein imagination that had taken over my life and I lived more in my dream world than in what some call the "real" world.

But a writer?

I realized the job of being a writer wouldn't be advertised in the local newspaper. Writers were refined gentlemen who inhabited a world of exclusive clubs, lived in elegant country houses, or sat in villas in Greece typing while their personal chef conjured up lunch in the kitchen. Or so I naively believed. Becoming a writer seemed about as mysterious as becoming an astronaut—and just as unattainable. So what I did was take my desire to become a writer and bundled it away into the mental equivalent of a cellar, locked the door, told no one. It was my secret.

Why I treated my ambition as something sordid, something that the world must not know about, I just haven't a clue. But like a mad scientist working away at his machine that will allow him to become master of the universe, I beavered away in complete secrecy.

SHE LOVES MONSTERS

Late at night I sat in bed and scribbled away. Or, rather, I allowed my great galumphing Frankenstein imagination to run amok across the page. The stories were undisciplined, badly spelt, horrendously punctuated. But they were imaginative in a dark and profoundly bizarre way.

Taming The Monster

So, I pursued the "One Thing."

Call it passion. Monomania. Obsession. But from around fourteen onwards I wrote night after night.

When my parents went to the shops I lugged out my father's typewriter, typed until I heard the car pull up in the drive, then hid the typewriter and pretended I'd been watching television or loafing on my bed. I sent out stories. They bounced back with rejection slips. I sent one to the editor of an audio anthology. He said my story about a man who had taken root in a cave and survived by drawing nutrients from the soil and the innocents he lured there was 'too far-fetched.' Later I read that the editor was jailed for fraud.

This world of writing was stranger than I'd imagined.

My family and friends would think me strange if I ever "came out" as a writer, I'd tell myself. So I kept my hunt for the "One Thing" a closely guarded secret.

And still I continued writing. Practicing. Practicing. Trying to tame my Frankenstein imagination at least a little so I could produce a story that would be more accessible. More saleable, too.

A Glimpse Of Eldorado

The years slipped by. I was twenty with a desk-job in local government (after I'd scraped up some academic qualifications, so I could pretend I was a paid-up member of the real world—yet my Frankenstein imagination still galumphed happily in the privacy of my skull. Like any good addict, I hid my vice well).

I still wrote. I still got rejection slips. I wrote *Hobscross*, a novel about a rock star who unlocks the secret of an ancient standing stone and must fight pagan warriors from the past. Publishers sent it back. One editor told me novel-writing was a ferociously competitive business, that I wouldn't earn any more than around $500 from a book, and maybe I'd be happier forgetting the whole thing.

But I kept going. My Frankenstein imagination was both a comfort and consummate tormentor. I wrote because I had to: plays, poetry, stories.

Then, just as I hit twenty-one, a wonderful thing happened. In a newsagent in my old hometown of Wakefield I came across a magazine called *Luddsmill*. It was a product of something I came to know as the small-press. And, by God, I think it saved my life.

I sent some anarchic poetry to the magazine. Andy Darlington, its editor, accepted it. That acceptance letter I carried around in my pocket for weeks. Suddenly the "One Thing" I'd been searching for was in sight.

I showed the letter to Janet (who I was just weeks away from marrying). She looked at me puzzled and asked, "What does it mean?"

It meant, I suppose, I was coming out to the world as a writer. I was beginning to admit to family and friends this is what I wanted to be. It seems strange to admit it now, but ripping off that shell of secrecy from myself was painful and strange and destabilizing somehow. Even writing this today, I can feel a grimace on my face. It was like forcing myself to walk naked down the high street. The parts of me I'd carefully concealed were now exposed.

But life had become easier. I was writing for the small press. I met editors, fellow writers. Those writers were just like me. Good God, I wasn't the only one, after all. Now *that* was a revelation.

Janet and I married. An unseasonable blizzard turned our whole world pristine white. That was symbolic somehow, like a new page waiting to be written on.

I worked harder than ever. I got into the habit of getting up early and writing before leaving for the day job. When I came home I wrote in the evenings, too. Janet was a marvel. When I doubted myself she

SHE LOVES MONSTERS

encouraged me; when I was moody she turned a blind eye. Together we'd bundle up manuscripts that she'd mail with a good luck kiss.

Steve Sneyd, a poet and writer, who I came to know well, saw one of my short stories in a magazine called *Back Brain Recluse* edited by Chris Reed. Writing to me, Steve said, "That's just the kind of thing Karl Edward Wagner is looking for. He edits *The Year's Best Horror*. Why not send a photocopy of the story to him? Oh, and be sure to include the publication and copyright details."

I respected Steve's judgment, but I'd never heard of Karl Edward Wagner, or the *Year's Best Horror*. Nevertheless, I copied the story and sent it, not even expecting a reply.

That was in the summer of 1985.

In January of 1986 I received the following letter from Karl Edward Wagner:

"Dear Simon,

You'll be pleased to learn that '...Beside the Seaside, Beside the Sea...' has made the final cut for YEAR'S BEST HOROR XIV. If the enclosed permission forms are acceptable, please sign them and return one copy to me.

Payment is on publication—usually October or November. I'll send you a contributor's copy of the book as soon as I can wrest a supply from DAW. Experience has shown that I have to do this myself if it's to be done. (*the text in Karl's letter slips here*)

(Missed the lever on that last paragraph or something.)

Also I'd be grateful if you would please supply me with some bits of personal information for use in my introduction—date and place of birth, background, other publication, the usual. I've been known to make it up as I go along otherwise.

Finally, in a never-ending struggle to read everything I can find I've managed to let the collection wait until the last possible moment. The book is due on

DAW's desk at the end of this month. So please get back to me on this as soon as you possibly can.

Best wishes for a productive and prosperous 1986.

Sincerely, Karl."

I was only going to quote an extract from the letter at first, but here it is in full. This was possibly one of the most important letters of my life. It brought me within touching distance of the "One Thing" for which I was searching.

My $50 advance arrived ten months later and I received my copy of the book a little after that.

The $50 paid for a couple of Chinese take-out meals and a few rounds of drinks. But I felt my career as a professional writer was now well and truly launched.

I only had to mention the sale to this prestigious anthology and editors telephoned me with acceptances for stories I'd submitted. At last! Things were starting to happen. Or so I hoped…

Frankenstein Still Unbound

Year's Best Horror XIV appeared when I was hitting my late twenties. Janet and I lived in our own modest house with a young son, Alex, soon to be joined by a daughter, Helen. Of course, the family continued to share their home with the great, galumphing Frankenstein imagination, too. And, yes, it was still unbound.

And there's plenty for my Frankenstein to feed on. The neighborhood is littered with history. I take my bike along a Roman road to see where Caesar's legions marched. The local churchyard is littered with fragments of skeletons from a thousand years of burials. You can pick knucklebones and shards of skull from the soil.

Not far from here, the fourteenth-century mystic Richard Rolle experienced his own strange Close Encounters of the numinous kind. An offshoot of the George Washington family lived just across the

SHE LOVES MONSTERS

road—their bones lie beneath medieval stone slabs that bear their Stars and Stripes coat of arms.

I was still writing hard.

My stories were now appearing on local radio (paycheck: $10) and in more editions of *The Year's Best Horror*. I met Karl Wagner (something I feel privileged to have done: the man's a legend). In a bar Karl made spontaneous royalty payments in beer to me and other *Year's Best* contributors. A little after that, my first collection of stories, *Blood & Grit*, appeared from BBR Books in 1990.

But still I had the day job, which I hated more and more. Frankenstein imagination galumphed yet more wildly.

Then, one morning, I woke up knowing the day had come, at last, to jump from that high wall.

Okay, so it wasn't a real wall; it was a metaphorical one. I felt as scared as that six-year-old on the demolition site did all those years ago, but I had to do it all the same.

I quit the day job and made that leap.

It was a long drop. Longer than I could have ever anticipated.

I completed a novel, *Nailed By The Heart*. Then I wrote *Blood Crazy*. Whereas *Nailed By The Heart* took around five years, *Blood Crazy* just erupted out of me over a space of three months or so. My Frankenstein imagination had been allowed off its leash properly for the first time, and, my God, in freedom it EXULTED.

Frankenstein imagination was happy now.

But life was hard. There was no money coming in to speak of. When times became harder I took a bank loan. I brewed my own beer, which must have worked out at a couple of cents per glass. I ordered more credit cards. I learnt to pay one using the other.

How those balances grew. But at least, for a while anyway, I managed to avoid making those stinging monthly payments.

An agent to whom I mailed my top copy of *Nailed By The Heart* left the agency. The manuscript vanished. With desperation tightening every muscle in my body to near snapping point I sent a carbon of the novel to UK publisher Hodder & Stoughton.

I also began a frantic mailing to a dozen different agents with the same line: "Do you want to represent me?" And back came the refusals.

I waited to hear from Hodder & Stoughton.

And the weeks passed.

Christmas came and went.

My savings were all gone.

Frankenstein imagination galumphed happy and free.

I sat in front of the computer, writing hard, waiting for the phone to ring, trying not to think about mortgage repayments or mounting bills, or the fact the children needed new clothes. My back muscles locked into a series of painful cramps. Stress was hitting my body good and hard.

At the end of February an agent telephoned out-of-the-blue, asking if I'd sold the novels I mentioned in my mail-shot. I said, "No."

The agent said, "I know the horror editor at Hodder. I'll give him a ring and find out what he thinks of the novel, if that's all right with you?"

I'd come this far without taking anything for granted. Trying not to think about what was happening to the manuscript, I returned to the computer. There I allowed Frankenstein imagination to galumph at will. Words poured out onto the hard disk.

The car needed a new muffler. I had no money. I left the car in the garden, so at least it wouldn't wake the dead.

March 1. Tuesday lunchtime. I'd put a pan of tomato soup on to warm. The telephone rang.

"Hello, Simon," the voice said, "Bob Tanner here at International Scripts. Look, Simon, I've just telephoned Nick Austin at Hodder & Stoughton..."

That's when fate did what it's apt to do. It took my life suddenly in a new direction. I was taking that step forward into the unknown again.

The voice continued: "...and he's wanting to make you an offer."

There was a kind of timelessness. I could hear the beat of the pulse in my neck. The world had gone faraway.

"Hello, Simon, are you still there?"

"Yes."

"I was saying that Hodder wants to make an offer."

"*Nailed By The Heart?*" was all I managed to say.

"No."

"Oh..."

"No, not just *Nailed By The Heart*. They want to buy *Blood Crazy*, too. What do you say to their offer?"

SHE LOVES MONSTERS

What could I say?

The six-year old me had been too afraid to jump off the high wall.

The thirty-six-year old me had at last plucked up courage to make that leap. At last I'd landed. It was terrifying. But I'd made it. I'd joined my gang. I was a professional writer.